Lifetime to Lifetime:
A Tale of Rebirth and Spiritual Awakening

Written by
Christopher S. Roman, Ph.D.

Adapted by:
Cynthia H. Roman, Ed.D.

ISBN 978-1-62806-267-0 (print | paperback)
ISBN 978-1-62806-268-7 (ebook)
ISBN 978-1-62806-269-4 (ebook)

Library of Congress Control Number 2020905001

Published by Salt Water Media
29 Broad Street, Suite 104
Berlin, MD 21811
www.saltwatermedia.com

Cover design by Salt Water Media: background image by
Unsplash user Patrick Fore, stock image purchased by
Cynthia Roman

Table of Contents

Acknowledgements

Chris Roman – my late husband, whose spiritual quest and intellectual curiosity led to this story. I hope with all my heart that I've done you justice.

Jim Wieboldt – my husband, who asks good questions, provides helpful feedback and hushes the dogs when I'm trying to write. I love you, Babe!

Mary Lib Morgan – my friend and editor, who helped me make sure I used dashes instead of hyphens, as well as a lot of other things! You never fail to be there when I need you.

Jeanne Schlesinger – my inspired and inspiring illustrator! Thank you for contributing your spirit and your talent.

Preface

Through the round of many births I roamed
without reward,
without rest,
seeking the house-builder.
Painful is birth
again & again.
House-builder, you're seen!
You will not build a house again.
All your rafters broken,
the ridge pole destroyed,
gone to the Unformed, the mind
has come to the end of craving.
— From *the Dhammapada,* by Gautama Buddha

In the world today, all of us struggle to find meaning. We try new jobs, different relationships, bigger homes – these pursuits are often exciting and challenging, but ultimately leave us still hungry. We try churches and religions, but may find that these, too, leave us feeling unsure. It's hard to accept church dogma if it doesn't match our own experience of the world. At some time in our lives, a crisis of meaning occurs. We have to make a painful admission to ourselves. We finally understand that there is nothing in the outside world that can give us the answers we seek or the happiness we long for.

Only when we've experienced this profound disappointment can we really begin again. Not finding meaning outside, we learn to turn inward. Slowly...gradually, we begin to explore the landscape of our own hearts and souls, and the answers that have eluded us all our lives start to emerge. Nothing is ever the same again.

This pattern of seeking meaning in the world, failing, and turning inward is a drama that has played out in billions of human lives through a million years of history. My late husband, Chris Roman, was on his own spiritual journey while he wrote the first draft of this story. When he died of leukemia in 2008, the manuscript lay unfinished on the shelf. Ten years later, remarried and pursuing a mindful retirement lifestyle, I decided to finish Chris's story. I had three goals: to seal his legacy, to embolden my own spiritual journey, and to inspire others' spiritual development. Like Chris, my inner work has been slow, arduous, and punctuated by episodes of anger, frustration, depression, and backsliding. I also felt unequal to my brilliant husband. My knowledge of Buddhism was nowhere near Chris' level of understanding. My practice of meditation has at times been more perfunctory than meaningful. So, I put the manuscript aside again while I wrote my first novel.

Surprisingly, writing fiction inspired me immensely. I felt newly empowered – both spiritually and mentally. Somehow, I knew that I was ready to do whatever it took to launch the story of Eric Hill and his brother, Sam, into the world. Much of the story was already complete and Chris's voice rings in every astonishing experience that Eric and Sam share. My job was to "round out" the rough edges, update the context, and bring more coherence to the story's progress. While Eric is a fictional character, he feels as real to me as he did to Chris. Eric represents the hope and promise of the inner journey.

This is a modern tale about a 12-year old boy who discovers that he has a mystical gift – a gift that transforms his life and the lives of his family and friends. I hope this story resonates in your own heart as it does in mine, and as it did in Chris' life. May this story stir a yearning for magic and meaning in your own life.

Chris' mystical life, like Eric's, was rooted in the Theravada Buddhist tradition. He practiced meditation several days a week and attended a 10-day Vipassana, (*meditation involving concentration on the body or its sensations, or the insight which this provides*) retreat each year. The retreats required waking up at 4 am, maintaining silence, and refraining from all the distractions of the outside world (i.e. no TV, cell phone, alcohol, tobacco, etc.). It was hard work, but Chris discovered a joy and a sense of peace that helped to sustain his spiritual journey for the rest of his "too short" life.

This story is not, by itself, an adequate guide for your spiritual journey, but it may inspire you to find your own teacher. Be careful, though, when you choose a teacher; it is not so easy to distinguish a guru from a pretender. Whatever path you choose, and whatever teacher you find —may you be happy, may you be free from harm, and may you discover your own truth.

Cynthia Roman, 2019
Christopher Roman, 2003

Chapter 1
Louisiana Bound

I seem to have loved you in numberless forms, numberless times...
In life after life, in age after age, forever.
My spellbound heart has made and remade the necklace of songs,
That you take as a gift, wear round your neck in your many forms,
In life after life, in age after age, forever.

— From *Unending Love* by Rabindranath Tagore

Three weeks ago, on a grey February morning, I sat at my kitchen table with my laptop and opened Google Maps. I've used Google Maps many times, but this was the first time I began plotting my car trip from California to Louisiana. As I looked at the interstates and alternative routes, I realized just how much time and money would be involved for such an ambitious trip. Just then, Cathy brought me a freshly brewed cup of coffee and, as she set the cup on the table next to my laptop, she peered into the screen.

"What are you doing?" she asked.

I sighed deeply because I knew this was a loaded question and how I chose to respond would make a big difference. I decided to delay what would most certainly be a difficult conversation.

"Oh, I was just looking at what would be involved in navigating a trip to Louisiana. I'd really like to talk with you more about it when you get home from work today. How does that sound to you?"

Cathy frowned and said, "Okay."

Before I could respond further, Cathy turned and went back to the bedroom to get ready for work.

Outside my bay window, the sun was hidden by a gathering thundercloud. Light rain pitter-pattered on my roof. In the distance, I saw my neighbor Judy on the sidewalk, wrestling to open her umbrella. She glared at the sky in defeat.

I've known Judy for ten years. And I know she gets angry when things aren't going her way. I stepped onto my porch, hoping to speak with her, but she disappeared around the corner. Glancing down at my pajamas and bare feet, I hesitated before stepping out into the quickening rain. I took three measured steps and tilted my face up toward the dark sky. With eyes shut, I could easily smell the rain and hear distant thunder. A minute later I was still motionless – my face, hair, and clothes were soaked. I could not recall feeling more alive.

When Cathy came home late in the afternoon, I sat down on our bed as she changed into her more casual clothes. I spoke to her of dark skies, my soaring spirits, and Louisiana. And I read to her from Eric's diary. I read the poem that had lifted me high in the past. Her response was slow and measured.

"Sam – it's amazing. Eric could see beyond this world to places we could only imagine. But this poem doesn't bring him back. Eric is dead. I'm sure the kid Eric describes in this poem is alive somewhere in Louisiana. But he's not Eric Hill. He has his own name and identity and life – we're not part of it."

I bristled at her words.

"I *am* a part of it! As are you! To deny that is to deny

everything we've learned, everything we know. This kid in Louisiana probably doesn't look or sound like Eric, but he *is* Eric in the only sense that really matters – the soul within him has lived before."

Cathy didn't answer – she sat silently, eyes downcast. I saw that I had been too harsh.

"Look, Cathy, by any kind of logic – you're right. My expectations may be completely dashed. I could waste many weeks trying to locate this kid. The poem has very little information to go on. And if I do find him, his parents could have me arrested for stalking him."

Cathy flashed an involuntary smile.

"But Cathy, this isn't about logic. It's about miracles. I can betray logic, but I can't betray a miracle."

I stood up, walked to the bedroom closet, and pulled out my large brown leather suitcase. Cathy stared, startled by my abrupt movement. I laid the suitcase on the bed and unzipped it.

"Don't go, Sam." And she began to cry. Her shoulders rose and fell as she wept.

I gathered her into my arms. Even as I held her, I thought, *If only she felt the way I do.*

The fact is, Cathy often doesn't feel as I do. The smell of rain is not the least bit interesting to her. Oil painting, which is her passion, is not particularly interesting to me. Dinner parties excite her, while I concoct excuses to leave early. She cries profusely during romantic movies, while I study the director's use of light and shadow.

In the first year of our relationship, I felt profoundly disappointed over the differences between us. Or perhaps more accurately, I was disappointed in *her* for not feeling as *I* did. Of course, I had very high expectations for a mate.

Having studied reincarnation for years, I expected to locate and reunite with the soulmate of my past lives. I wanted Cathy to be the one woman I was destined to be with.

As our differences emerged, I lamented. Cathy was beautiful, smart, eloquent, and full of compassion for anyone in trouble. I was drawn to her for all that, but sorry that she wasn't more. I was still convinced that this other woman was waiting somewhere for me – the woman I would grow old with; the woman who would share with me the thrill of a morning thunderstorm, the joy of miracles, the excitement of love renewed.

In 2010, three days before Christmas, my idea of soulmates changed for good. Cathy had just hung up the phone after hearing of her father's death, and I cradled her as she wept. I was grateful that I could be present for her, to be able to offer her my support. And I also saw that to care for her required that I *not* be enmeshed in her grief. The fact that I could feel happy as she wept made all things possible between us. We were soul- mates after all. Soulmates living in separate streams. When one sinks, the other offers a hand. We take turns lifting each other from the mud.

On this still grey February afternoon, it was my turn to do the lifting. Cathy blotted her eyes with a tissue, but they still watered. I started to give in to her pleas, but stopped mid-sentence. She was asking too much of me. I pulled my arm from her shoulder and moved away slightly.

"Cathy, I've learned a lot in in my life – but knowledge is worthless unless it's used. In Louisiana, I can use a lifetime of knowledge. I can fulfill a goal made six hundred years ago in the mountains of Tibet. I can start a miracle in motion."

Cathy nodded, rose slowly from the bed, and went downstairs. At least she had stopped crying. A minute later,

I heard her setting up her easel and canvas. Soon she would be immersed in her painting.

I began tossing clothes into my suitcase. I kept adding and subtracting jeans, t-shirts, and sweaters – unsure of how much to take. Would I be gone three days or three months? I removed a wool sweater and everything else that wasn't easily washable at a laundromat. I culled clothes that I could wear in layers to accommodate changing seasons.

As I rolled up a pair of white cotton socks, my body convulsed, momentarily taking my breath away. I sat down hard on the bed.

Eric again. This physical sensation happens to me every few weeks. A grief so intense, it shakes my body. It's as though he had just died. When it comes, I've learned not to fight it. Grief, it seems, has to run its own course. This time, thankfully, it was short-lived. I dispelled it with a simple heartfelt whisper.

"Eric, my teacher – I'm coming."

An old proverb says "When the student is ready, the teacher will appear." I was fifteen and longing for answers when my teacher appeared. I had spent every day with Eric since the day he was born. I loved him for his laughter, his bright eyes, and his absolute trust in me. But when Eric was ten years old, I saw something completely different in those bright eyes. I saw the teacher that I had longed for.

At ten, Eric was only starting to develop the deep wisdom that would someday draw disciples from around the world. But his nascent wisdom was deep enough to capture me. I recognized my unshakeable belief that I had been born for a single purpose – to follow him.

Years later, as a religion student at Wickham College, I learned I was not the first person to be captured by the wisdom of a child. Ancient Buddhist scriptures tell of spiritual masters as young as seven. Their bodies were young, but their souls were very old. Their wisdom was an accumulation of many past lives.

The diary Eric left is a blue leather-bound journal Mom gave him for his twelfth birthday. The pages are unruled, which suited Eric's penchant for sketching with pencils. I found the book in a footlocker, in the basement, behind a stack of old furniture. I had opened the footlocker several times before - it was full of holly wreaths, sleigh bells, and Christmas lights; just some of the holiday decorations that Eric would string all over the house each December. I clearly remember his excitement every year as he ran down the stairs to the basement, simultaneously announcing his decorating intentions. Cathy and I didn't bother much with Christmas, and I only opened the trunk when enough time had passed for me to forget what was in it. Each time I rediscovered its contents, I closed it and shoved it further back in the corner.

Three weeks ago, I finally pulled it to the center of the basement floor, underneath the ceiling lamp, and emptied it. I had decided to donate the contents to the Salvation Army. Eric's blue journal was there at the bottom. As I opened it for the first time, my hands shook.

That shabby old book means more to me now than a footlocker of gold. Its cover is stained and torn. Its numbered pages are dense with scribbled words, half-finished sketches, and odd bits of poetry. And on page 114 is a sparkling jewel. In a rhymed poem just four stanzas in length, Eric tells of his next life, his new parents, and his future home. Just one page, written in pencil. Sixteen lines of poetry that renewed my life.

Finally settling on the clothes I would take, I closed the suitcase and shoved it back under the bed. I pulled Eric's diary from the top drawer of my dresser and headed downstairs, where I could still hear the sounds of Cathy painting with vigorous strokes of her brush.

I held the diary open to page 114.

"Read it once yourself, Cathy."

I waited a long minute. She read it several times, then stood up and wiped her hands on her smock.

"Sam, we're supposed to get married in June. That's my miracle. I've sent out invitations to all our friends. Now what? Instead of getting married you're going to trek across America looking for ghosts?"

I reached across to take her hand.

"Babe, I'm certainly not going to miss my own wedding. I'll be back long before June."

When she didn't answer, I squeezed her hand and went outside. Reclining on the front porch swing, I paged through Eric's diary once again. In the midst of all the jumbled thoughts that filled the pages, I was hoping for another jewel.

Forty-five minutes later, Cathy came to join me. Ignoring my invitation to sit next to me, she took a facing chair, the now setting sun just over her right shoulder.

"Sam, a lot of people believe in reincarnation, but that doesn't mean they try to find their loved ones after death. When your parents died, you didn't roam the country trying to find them again."

"My parents didn't leave a diary telling me where to look."

Cathy exhaled slowly and reached into her purse. She pulled a business card from her wallet, and looked at it for a moment before handing it to me.

"Sam, I want you to do something for me before we get

married – and before you take off. Talk to this woman. Just a few sessions."

I turned the card over.

Sheila M. Andrews, MD
General Psychiatry
St. Luke's Doctors Center
316 Eucalyptus Drive, Suite 112
Santa Rosa, California 91305

Cathy continued.

"Sam, when I had my physical in November, my blood pressure was off the chart. I didn't tell you because I didn't want to worry you. Dr. Summers said that planning a new job and a marriage at the same time was a dangerous mix. He prescribed something for me, but he also recommended I see Dr. Andrews to work on my 'coping skills.' I've been taking the medication, but never called the psychiatrist. But I saved her card, just in case."

I paused, letting her admission sink in. "Cathy, I'm hurt that you didn't tell me you were so stressed out. We can talk about that later."

I paused again and continued.

"There is nothing this woman can possibly do for me! I'm not stressed out. Quite the opposite, in fact. I can't recall feeling better than I do today."

Cathy lowered her eyes and didn't reply. She didn't have to. This was the best offer I was going to get from her today. I took it.

Using the kitchen phone, I called Dr. Andrews at home while Cathy watched. I made an appointment for three o'clock the next afternoon. After I hung up, I was no longer exactly sure whether I was lifting Cathy from the mud or she was lifting me.

Chapter 2
Dreams and Psychotherapy

Once a dream did weave a shade
O'er my angel-guarded bed,
That an emmet lost its way
Where on grass methought I lay.

— From *A Dream* by William Blake

On Thursday, I arrived fifteen minutes early at Dr. Andrews' office. The waiting room was a little too feminine for my taste. Wallpaper covered with rosebuds, lace curtains, and slender chairs that I feared would break under my weight. I chose the chair in the far corner of the waiting room, by the window and next to the potted palm tree. It was also situated the furthest from Dr. Andrew's private office door. This was calculated – I wanted to see how, after she opened her office door, she would negotiate the physical distance between us. Would she greet me from eight feet away, standing in her office doorway? Or would she walk to me, perhaps with her hand outstretched? I wasn't sure what it would mean to me if she did or didn't, but I knew it would

mean something. Eric used to tell me that you can never truly understand another until you see them tested. I'm not sure I fully grasped Eric's meaning, but I have applied his advice ever since. Whether it's Cathy or the neighbors, I find myself devising subtle little tests, just to see how they will respond. When dining out with friends, I sometimes grab the check first and insist on paying for everyone. It's not that I'm really so generous – it's just that I'm curious how the others will respond. Will they graciously accept my offer? Will they insist on dividing the check? Or will they counteroffer, insisting that they, not I, should pay for everyone? Perhaps it's all a little mischievous on my part, but I still hear Eric's words in my head – "You never truly understand another until you see them tested."

I sat slowly in my chosen chair and rocked gently back and forth, testing its strength. Once comfortable, I saw that all the magazines stacked on the side table were feminine – Glamour, Vogue, House and Garden. What were male patients supposed to read? With reluctance, I began flipping through an April issue of Glamour with Millie Bobby Brown on the cover. I was a big fan of the Netflix series, Stranger Things, and this young star, who had superpowers on the show, interested me. After stopping briefly at three advertisements for women's underwear, I became absorbed in the interview with Brown.

Then I noticed I wasn't alone. Sheila Andrews had somehow entered the waiting room without my hearing her. She was standing quietly just three feet away, hands clasped easily in front of her, her face displaying a smile that bore just a hint of mischief. I flushed and tossed the magazine aside. Her smile broadened – "You're welcome to take it home with you if you like."

"No." I pulled at my collar. "No thank you." I stumbled to my feet and shook her hand. Once on my feet, I could see that she was as tall as I – six feet. Her handshake was firm and confident – the word masculine came to mind. This was off to an awkward start. She had disrupted my test.

The armchairs in her office were sturdier – big heavy leather-covered affairs with brass riveting not unlike my favorite TV chair at home. I sank comfortably into one and she occupied its twin, facing me directly. I enjoyed the first few seconds of eye contact. I studied her face more closely, her eyes and mouth. I could see now she was young - maybe too young. Definitely under thirty. She was also very attractive - silky skin, a sharp jaw line, and a perfect nose. Her tailored blouse and slacks looked expensive. She wore her auburn hair in a bun, and she seemed very relaxed.

I flushed with the realization that I had been staring at her an inappropriately long time. I glanced away quickly, feigning interest in her floor lamp. It looked new – as did all the office furnishings; no trace of dust anywhere. This explained the ease with which I got a next-day appointment. Sheila must be recently established.

With her notepad resting on her lap, she watched me expectantly, never averting her gaze. She was waiting for me to speak. My hands started to perspire as I realized that over a minute had elapsed between us with no words exchanged.

I suppose psychiatrists are trained to do just that – watch their patients and wait for them. It's their version of understanding people by seeing them tested. When I realized that I was the one being tested, I resumed my silent study of her face.

A few seconds of silence seemed like days, and I gave up. I started with a nearly incoherent string of admissions, excuses, and denials. I told her I had come as a favor to my fiancé. I told her that I had lived my whole life right here in Santa Rosa. I told her about my mom and dad, and about my brother Eric's life and death. I talked about the diary, told her of my travel plans, and of Cathy's disappointment. Sheila was taking notes rapidly, and I began to feel important.

Then she stopped me. "Let's back up. You said that Eric died thirteen years ago *for the last time.* Do you mean there were other times that he died?"

"Yes – he began dying when he was twelve, and he died almost every day for three years. Then Chandy, a monk we know, told Eric to stop dying and practice deep meditation instead. Eric trusted Chandy and did as he was told. A few months later, Chandy begged Eric to die one more time. He said, "You must die so someone else can be rescued from death.""

"And, of course, Chandy was right – Eric died, and in so doing, a 10-year old boy narrowly escaped death. Then, ten years later, Eric was diagnosed with anaplastic astrocytoma. He averted the last phase of the disease by ending his own life. I suppose you could call it suicide – but I call it supreme courage. Eric sat cross-legged on the floor, said goodbye to me, closed his eyes, took one last breath and died for the last time on January 11, 2006. It was a week after his twenty-eighth birthday."

Sheila nodded and made a note. I could see that her lips had tightened. The easy and relaxed smile had vanished. Now it was just silent attention on me.

Feeling suddenly less important, I kept talking anyway. When I reached the part about Michael, she stopped me again.

"You called Michael a *Deva.* What is that?"

"Devas are intelligent beings," I answered. "– much more intelligent than humans, actually. They live in a different, largely invisible realm. But Devas become visible when they choose. And a very few humans are able to see Devas all the time, regardless of the Devas' intentions. It takes a special eye to see a Deva that is trying to be invisible.

But seen or unseen, Devas commonly become attached to a particular human. The Deva is acutely aware of karmic fields, and will sometimes stumble on a human with whom they feel an intense karmic connection. Once a Deva feels that connection, it will work ceaselessly to protect the chosen one from harm and evil. In medieval folklore, such Devas are called *Guardian Angels*."

Sheila, checking her notes, asked "What about the Deva you call Michael? Did you actually see him?"

"I saw him twice – I remember both occasions vividly. I get so annoyed with people who say they've seen a Deva, and when you press them, they talk about seeing amorphous shapes bathed in haze or light. It usually turns out they don't know what they saw.

But with me, there's no doubt what I saw. I looked right into Michael's ancient eyes – he's over five thousand years old – and I felt enveloped by his love. I'll never forget it."

I shifted my talk back to Eric, describing the church he founded and the charities he supported. At some point, Sheila stopped taking notes.

When we had ten minutes left, she stopped me once again. It was now her turn to talk.

"I have to tell you, Sam, I've never heard of your brother, Eric. I gather from what you say that he was quite the celebrity here, but I grew up in Connecticut. I don't think Eric's reputation traveled that far east."

As Sheila continued to talk, I flushed and felt my body tense defensively. I was embarrassed at my own naiveté.

It was now clear that Sheila Andrews had believed little of what I had told her. And why should she? She had never met Eric or even heard of him. From her viewpoint, the last hour had consisted of nothing more than the ranting of a delusional patient. Her interest in what I had said was clinical, not collegial. I now wanted to escape.

Sheila stopped talking, closed her note pad, and sat up straight. I prepared to listen.

"You obviously loved your brother, Sam, and that's laudable. It's also appropriate. But your feelings for him go beyond love. You think of Eric as a God."

She leaned forward, as if to share a secret. "He wasn't a God, Sam. He was a person like you and me. He had unique qualities - sure, but so do we all."

I bit my lower lip and nodded, thinking to myself, *Dr. Andrews, you haven't a clue.*

She walked to her desk, and pulled a sketch pad from the drawer. "This is for you. Right now, it's just blank pages. I want you to write your story – the story you just told me. Getting it down on paper will help us to see things differently."

I stood and accepted it, trying to appear humble. I wondered at the same time how I could avoid returning to this place. I realized that I couldn't – not without upsetting Cathy.

If the last hour with Dr. Andrews had been a test, I lost. I would have to return – would have to spend another hour with someone who thought I was a lunatic. Sheila was still talking, but I had tuned her out. I tried to imagine her real, unspoken thoughts:

He seemed so normal when I met him in the waiting room. I was expecting a middle-aged man with ev-

eryday marital difficulties. But no! I get a raving lu-
natic who sees ghosts and worships his dead brother!

I shook her hand graciously and accepted the sketch pad. Whether Sheila believed me or not, I decided to play along.

"There are no constraints," she said. "You can write sideways or upside down. Or you can draw pictures."

I nodded, knowing that when I got home, the sketch pad was going in the closet. I would write on my computer, the way I liked. I started writing after dinner that night, and didn't stop until 3:00 am, when fatigue set in. I awoke at eight, still slumped over my desk.

Three days later, at our second appointment, I gave Sheila fifty typed pages. And I talked tearfully about the death of my parents.

The following week, when I entered Sheila's office, I saw the pages of my journal spread across her desk, the margin of every page colored in green ink with her handwritten comments.

I tilted my head toward the desk. "Looks like you've been doing some reading."

She glanced behind. "I like what you've written so far, Sam. You have a talent for journaling. Your story pulled me in. I wrote down some ideas – just little suggestions for things you might want to add."

During that third session, I talked about Triple Refuge, the church and charity that Eric and I founded. At the end of the session, I gave her sixty more typed pages and gratefully accepted her mark-ups from the previous week. I was feeling important again.

As we made the trade, she hesitated. "Don't forget yourself, Sam. When you write about Eric, you seem as invisible as a Deva. Let me see more of you."

That same night, I had a dream:

> *I am teaching a college religion class. The kids look like freshmen or sophomores. They also look distracted; they're whispering to each other, passing notes, and, in the back of the room, a safe distance from me, one student is napping with his head on his desk.*
>
> *In contrast, I am absorbed. Today's topic is mysticism, and I intend to do more than talk. My voice rises and I wave my arms:*
>
> *"What **would** it mean if you could see behind the veil of appearances where reality starts? If you could see as the ancient mystics saw?"*
>
> *The kids aren't responding yet. I walk over to the blackboard and reach up toward one corner. My hand doesn't just grab the edge of the board; it actually penetrates the board, as though it were entering a pool of water. Space and time ripple as I peel back the fabric of reality. I hold in my hand a corner of the universe - torn away to see beyond. Bright hypnotic light streams through the opening.*
>
> *I turn to the class in triumph. "What **does** it mean?"*
>
> *My students are stunned. It takes several seconds for them to respond. The blonde kid in the front row starts to applaud, and everyone joins in. I'm embarrassed when the applause doesn't stop. I let go of the board, allowing the breach to close and the light to cease. I survey the room. I now have my students' complete attention.*

When I awoke, it took a minute to recognize my own bedroom. I reached in the closet for the sketch pad that Sheila gave me and began writing down the details of my dream while they were fresh and lucid. I used to have lucid dreams all the time, when I was in my twenties and thirties. But this was my first lucid dream in many years.

At Wickham College I studied Carl Jung and came to appreciate the importance of dreams. Jung saw dreams as windows into the soul, and he recorded and analyzed his own dreams and those of his patients. That was the year I began keeping a dream journal. I wanted to be like Jung.

Once at breakfast, Eric saw me writing and asked to see my journal. His face broke into a wide smile as he read.

"You're doing exactly the right thing, Sam. Listen carefully to your dreams. They're the possibilities your unconscious is struggling with to make real. Each dream is an opportunity for us to grow in unexpected ways."

At my next appointment with Dr. Andrews, I gave her my final sixty pages, including the record of my lucid dream. She leafed through, stopping for a minute to read my dream. She smiled as she read – a sweet smile that conveyed a hint of vulnerability that I hadn't seen before.

"What do you think it means?" she asked.

"Oh, I think it means that, deep down, I want to be a teacher. A teacher of things that matter. I've had similar dreams before."

"And so? Are you going to follow your brother's advice? And use the dream as an opportunity for growth? You could make your dream real if you wanted."

"No I couldn't." I rubbed my hands together, noticing that they were sweating.

"After Eric died, I tried. I tried to run Triple Refuge alone.

But I failed – I couldn't teach the way Eric taught. And I felt foolish for even trying."

"What makes you believe you failed?" Sheila pulled her chair closer to mine.

"Triple Refuge wasn't successful because of anything Eric Hill *said*, or anything he *did*. It was successful because of who he *was*. Eric was the teaching. People listened to Eric's words, but that's not what made them come, and that's not what brought them back. Eric had a presence that could penetrate souls. He captivated people; changed people. People would be transformed at first encounter. Within ten minutes I saw people wiping tears from their eyes, after fifteen minutes many would stop holding back and let their tears flow.

And at the end of the hour, they would be different. When they left, their posture was straighter, more open. The tension in their faces was gone. Arriving as strangers, people would depart with arms entwined.

I remember speaking with a first-timer after Eric had finished. Shaken, he told me that Eric's talk was the most moving experience of his life. Of his entire life! And this was a man in his sixties with grandchildren, a man who had made spiritual pilgrimages throughout the world. And Eric was a twenty-three-year-old who had never gone to college, never had children, and had never left the United States. There's no way I could do what Eric did. Because I can't be who he was."

Sheila stopped writing on her pad and looked up at me. "And why should you? You're not Eric Hill – you're Sam Hill. You have your own presence and your own power. Maybe you don't draw large crowds, but people love you just the same. They don't measure you against your brother, and neither should you."

Sheila's pep talk worked. I smiled. Maybe therapy wasn't so bad after all.

At my fourth and last appointment yesterday, I handed this completed journal to Sheila. I thought it odd when she laid it on her desk without looking at it or me.

Still averting her eyes, she asked, "Do you have a photograph of your brother?"

I fumbled through my wallet and pulled out a well-worn picture from 1994. She studied it intensely, breathing quickly and looking somewhat distressed.

"What's wrong?"

She handed the photograph back to me, leaned back in her chair and stared at the ceiling.

"I had my first lucid dream last night. I'm still feeling a bit shaken," she said. "I dreamed I was trapped in a labyrinth. Intersecting walls of tall green hedges in every direction. I was walking and walking, completely lost. But I actually wasn't upset. Instead, I was absorbed in the vivid details all around me. I could see each individual leaf on the hedges and smell their scent! I could feel air against my face. I've never had a dream like that.

Then I started to worry because it was getting dark and I didn't know the way out. I quickened my pace. The more I walked, taking one sharp turn after another, the more anxious I became. Then I saw someone walking in front of me. He had on a hooded robe, like a monk's robe, and he also was walking quickly. I struggled to catch up, but no matter how fast I ran, he seemed to be moving faster. I finally called out. "Wait! I need your help!" But he kept walking.

Then I got the strongest feeling that the person in the robe was you! So, I start shouting as loudly as I could -

"Sam! Wait up!"

Sheila stopped for a moment, and then closed her eyes – as if reliving the dream.

"The robed figure stops and turns. He pulls his hood down. He is gorgeous! Not physically gorgeous, although he is quite handsome. It's a radiant, spiritual kind of beauty – it's in his eyes. He says, 'You must know my brother. How is he?'

I can't answer. I wake up struggling. I don't want to wake up. I want to stay in the dream; I want to return. I sit up in bed, my fists clenched, hating the feeling of being awake.

All day I've been thinking about that dream. I remember his hair, his eyes, his lips and teeth. I was so close I could smell him. When I saw your photo, it didn't surprise me. In fact, I think I would have been surprised if the person in my dream *wasn't* Eric Hill.

Sheila leaned back in her chair and looked up at the ceiling, and then back at me.

"Sam, this is new territory for me."

She looked at me with a tender smile of surrender.

"I guess this means we're done with therapy, Sam. I can no longer be objective in your case. There won't be a charge for today."

I felt not only important, but rather proud. Just four weeks ago, Dr. Sheila Andrews thought I was a nut. And now she was grasping my hands in gratitude. Her hands were soft and yielding, feminine.

As I turned to go, she made a final request. "Call me when you return, Sam. I want to know what happens."

I grinned. "You'll get a trip report. And who knows, maybe I'll bring back the man of your dreams."

That afternoon, I pulled my duffel bag out of the closet

and resumed packing. Cathy watched me from the doorway. Her body was relaxed, her eyes happy. I walked to her and kissed her on the ear, allowing my lips to linger a while. She whispered, "When you come back, I'm going to marry you."

The last three weeks served me well. I wrote this journal. With the help of the internet, I refined my trip plans. And I discovered that Sheila Andrews was wrong. Psychotherapy didn't help me see my life or Eric's life differently. If this journal helped anyone to see life differently, it was Sheila. I think she allowed herself, for the first time, to believe in miracles.

Chapter 3
Life with Eric Hill

Deep, indeed, is this dependent origination.
It is through not understanding and penetrating it that people
become entangled like a tangled ball of threads.
—From *Long discourse No. 15* by Gautama Buddha

I guess it's commonplace for children to view the arrival of a new brother or sister with suspicion. After all, the baby is bound to displace the other children as the center of the parents' attention. When Eric arrived, I gave up my play-room – it was converted to a nursery. And I lost the exclusive attention of my parents, which I had enjoyed immensely. Like all five-year-olds, I was selfish. Five-year-olds are *supposed* to be selfish – sharing and generosity come later as part of the child's developmental process.

Which is why my own reaction to my mom's pregnancy with Eric surprised them and me. I didn't feel threatened or suspicious. I can only remember excitement. Each evening Mom invited me to put my hand on her stomach and feel Eric kicking inside. I don't remember clearly all my feelings, but I think even then I was feeling a deep connection with this unborn being. Instead of feeling a kick, I felt a reassuring touch – as if Eric was stroking my hand through my mother's flesh.

The feeling persisted when Mom brought red-faced Eric home from the hospital on a rainy Wednesday morning. She was surprised at my eagerness to help her. I sat by Eric's crib and read stories to him; I warmed his bottle and fed him. I left it to Mom to deal with his dirty diapers, but I helped with everything else. My friends thought me strange when I declined to play soccer. They couldn't imagine why I would voluntarily babysit rather than play with them. Thinking back to this time, I can't explain why I was so drawn to my baby brother. Nothing else came close to the need I had at the time to love and care for him.

Although Mom was initially delighted that I wanted to help, eventually even she became concerned that I was avoiding children of my age group. She and Dad pushed me into clarinet lessons after school, and then into the elementary school band. In fourth grade, they pushed me to join the school soccer team. I argued with my parents at first, but I eventually yielded to their pressure. I actually became quite competitive on the soccer field and was named first chair in the wind instruments section of the band.

Eric also adapted easily to my growing absence. In kindergarten, he became fast friends with six other neighborhood kids. I still remember their names: Jesse Lynch, Liam Sanders, Amanda Jones, Paul Lyon, Lisa Green, and Melissa Knox. After school, they all gathered with Eric in our basement. Gradually the basement was transformed into Eric's clubhouse. It was decorated with his posters of Michael Jackson, Journey, and David Bowie. It reverberated from his record player booming out "Billie Jean." And it was the site for dozens of improvised games. When I got home from school, I could hear the revelry in the basement and I would feel left out. The difference in our ages now felt like a barrier – I couldn't go downstairs; I wasn't suited for their children's games. Furtively, I would crack the basement door and watch as long as I dared. I marveled at the extent to which Eric controlled the room. His six friends seemed content to let Eric devise the games, figure out the rules, and direct the action. It was Eric's club and they were happy just to be members. They would play nonstop until six p.m., when the phone would start ringing. Mothers wanted their kids home for dinner.

Sometimes, in spite of Eric's best efforts, I would see one of his friends stomp angrily up the stairs and out of our house. Eric's clubhouse would then become quiet. Perhaps Eric and his friends were trying to figure out what went wrong. When things went awry in the club, Eric blamed himself. He would ask me for advice. *What should he tell Jesse to smooth things over? And why did she get angry in the first place?* I found it interesting that it was never Eric that got angry. He shouldered blame, sought out advice, but never lost his temper.

Mom and Dad actually worried about Eric because of this. They worried that his inability to express anger was symptomatic of some kind of developmental problem. I overheard them discussing whether to send him to a child psychiatrist for evaluation. But they didn't. They decided that complaining to a shrink that their kid wasn't angry enough was a little too strange.

I wonder what the shrink's diagnosis would have been. Flat affect? In a young kid? One thing I know for sure; his absence of anger wasn't just a temporary phase in his development. For the rest of Eric's life, I never saw him get angry. He would forcefully confront people when he felt they were hiding their feelings or needs. He would talk sternly when he felt someone was being unfair or cruel. But he didn't lose his temper. I don't think he had a temper to lose.

I had a temper. When I was eight and didn't get the new bike I wanted for my birthday, I stomped off to my room, slammed my door, and locked it tight. I screamed at my parents countless times, held my breath till my face turned red, stomped my feet till the walls shook. But I didn't stay angry – Eric would seek me out and ask me what was going on. I never had an answer that made any sense – to him or me. So, I would let the anger go. By the time I was ten, I was losing my temper less frequently. I was trying to emulate my little brother.

When he was ten and I was fifteen, I took Eric fishing. We both had fished with Dad before, but this was the first time for just the two of us. We fastened our rods and reels to the back of our bikes, and pedaled six miles to Sandy Mile Creek.

Measured by fishes caught, the six miles to Sandy Mile were not worthwhile. We rarely caught anything and, when we did, it wasn't big enough to keep. But then nobody really goes fishing to catch fish. People go fishing to be alone and connect with themselves. Or they go fishing to connect with others. Sitting quietly by still waters under a setting sun – there's nothing else to do.

And so it was for Eric and me. We caught no fish, but we had hours to talk. Thinking that Eric was now old enough to explain himself, I asked, "Eric, how come I've never seen you get mad?"

Eric stared pensively into the creek, as if digesting the question. When he looked back up at me, I was surprised that his eyes were moist with emotion.

"For one thing, it seems to me that anger is just illogical. How often does anger get people what they want? Just about never! In fact, it does the opposite. Also, when you get angry, you can be pretty sure somebody will get their feelings hurt and maybe the friendship will never be the same."

I couldn't help but try to refute my little brother.

"But Eric, everybody gets angry. If someone hurts you, takes something of yours, says something insulting – it's only natural to get angry in response."

Eric felt a tug on his fishing rod, and carefully reeled in a discarded plastic bag green with algae. He pulled it from his hook and set it aside.

"When I see an angry person, I don't see the anger. I see the fear that the anger is trying to conceal. It's really not hard to see. It's right beneath the surface. Remember when you got angry over the bike you wanted for your birthday? It hurt me to see you that way. I could see that it wasn't really about the bike. It was about something much more important. For a little kid, birthday presents feel like symbols of love. 'My parents love me because they gave me this.' But the opposite can also be true in the kid's mind: 'My parents didn't give me what I asked for; they must not love me.' When Mom and Dad didn't buy the bike you wanted, the most frightening possibility in the universe suddenly becomes very real. 'Maybe they don't love me after all.'

"That's the scary story children all over the world tell themselves all the time. It's also the same scary story adults tell themselves. Getting angry is one way we protect ourselves from the unthinkable. Anger slams the book shut and gets the scary story out of our head."

"But Eric, everyone can't be like you. *I* can't be like you. I feel what I feel. In certain predicaments I get angry. It's not something I consciously choose. It just happens. It's the same with all my emotions – sadness, envy, loneliness; they come when they will – I have no say about it."

Eric smiled through his wet eyes.

"These emotions don't arise from nothing. Life is about

figuring out what's underneath the emotions. I can see that most of my difficulties are rooted in some underlying fear. The way out of my difficulties is to attack the root cause. If I can become as fearless as the saints – so fearless that I don't pull back even at the point of my own death – then the root is destroyed. Without the root, anger cannot arise; disappointment cannot arise; and jealousy cannot arise. Without anger, disappointment, and jealousy clouding my vision, I can see who I really am. I can see who other people are."

Eric gazed out at the creek, showing no inclination to continue the conversation. I followed his gaze, and felt that I was seeing the green water, the muddy red earth at water's edge, and the dry brush along the bank all for the first time.

Neither Eric nor I caught a fish that Sunday. It was, by most standards, an ordinary day. But something significant shifted within me. As we biked home that afternoon, with the wind against our faces and Eric in the lead, I felt a hollow ache in my chest. And instinctively, I knew what it was going to take to fill me. I wanted to learn what he knew. I still didn't know how he knew. But I was determined to find out, and learn it for myself.

Years later, as a religion student at Wickham College, I read the classic Buddhist texts. The Buddha taught that all human troubles arise from a process called "dependent origination." When oil and wick are present, a flame can arise; when either is absent, the flame ceases. The Buddha taught that all human miseries can be traced just so. Working backwards through the chain of dependent origination, they all have their origin with an incipient wrong belief.

Ten-year-old Eric Hill's explanation of anger was uncannily close to the Buddhist scriptural explanation. Of course, in future years, the mystery was solved. Eric wasn't untrained at all. He was what the Buddhists call an "old soul" – someone who has worked diligently for many lifetimes, seeking the ultimate release. According to Buddhist lore, these old souls draw on the wisdom and virtues they have accumulated in past lives. It's not that they remember the events of their past lives – although Eric eventually did. It's that the so-called *paramis*, or perfections, have accumulated across many lifetimes. At an unconscious level, these paramis feed the intuition of old souls.

As I later discovered, Eric was an *ancient* soul, one the Buddhists call a *Sakadagami*, or a once-returner. According to Buddhist scriptures, a Sakadagami will undergo only one more human birth. In the next life, he or she will conquer the last fetters that trap the soul. In a single moment, he or she will become an *Arahat*, a saint. During the life of the last Buddha (around 500 BCE), thousands of men and women approached him with only a 'little dust on their eyes.' They were old souls with strong paramis, and they were ripe for complete enlightenment. Sometimes a single sentence from the mouth of the Buddha would be all that was required to push them into eternity.

The Buddha presented the Ten Perfections to Sariputta, his closest disciple. In the Theravada tradition, it is believed everyone must cultivate these ten paramis over many lifetimes to create the conditions for eventual enlightenment.

Original Pali	English Translation
Dana	Generosity
Sila	Virtue
Nekkhamma	Renunciation
Panna	Wisdom or Discernment
Viria	Energy
Khanti	Patience
Adhitthana	Determination
Sacca	Truthfulness
Upekkha	Equanimity
Metta	Loving Kindness or Goodwill

Chapter 4
Cracking Knuckles and Stopping Hearts

They say miracles are past; and we have our
philosophical persons, to make modern and familiar
things supernatural and causeless.

— From *All's Well that Ends Well* by William Shakespeare

I've noticed that adolescent boys revel in displays of bodily functions – belching loudly, farting, and cracking knuckles. In 1990, Eric could neither belch nor fart nor crack, but he was the star of seventh grade health class when he made his heart stop. Mrs. Rupert, the health teacher, had set up an oscilloscope to let her students see their own heartbeats. She had volunteers come up front, and she taped a sensor over the artery in their neck. The rhythm of each student's

pulse was displayed on the screen. She told each volunteer to breathe deeply, visualize a peaceful place, and relax the muscles in their body. Following Mrs. Rupert's instructions, most of the kids were able to visibly slow their pulse. A few of the students, apparently anxious over the wires dangling over their neck, were unable to relax. And one student's pulse increased steadily the longer she was hooked up. Mrs. Rupert was annoyed by all the aberrations in her experiment. She attached the sensor to her own neck and showed everyone how the process was supposed to occur.

Then it was Eric's turn. Eric took the chair and, after being wired, closed his eyes and leaned back. The display of heart rhythm became very slow and, after 15 seconds, it stopped. Mrs. Rupert thought the wire had come loose, and she checked both ends. When she told Eric to open his eyes, he didn't respond. Then she saw that Eric wasn't breathing. She reached over and touched his temple. There was no pulse and his skin was cold.

Mrs. Rupert screamed and fell from her chair, whereupon Eric blinked, gasped for air, and started rubbing his arms. The class was in chaos, with several students crying uncontrollably. The principal was summoned, but fifteen minutes later Mrs. Rupert and her class had regained their composure. Mrs. Rupert glared at Eric, now back in his seat, as if this was all his fault. She put her equipment away, told the class to study for the next day's nutrition test, and went to the principal's office to file a report. She never mentioned the incident again.

Mr. Martin, the principal, called Dad that evening to tell him what had happened that day at school. He assured Dad that the equipment had malfunctioned, not Eric's heart. Dad called Eric up from the basement – not sure whether to hug him or lecture him. When confronted, Eric shrugged his shoulders, feigned disinterest, and said that Mr. Martin was probably right. When Mom got home, Dad told her about the phone call. She was perplexed, called Eric back up from the basement, and checked his pulse with her wristwatch. "It's completely normal," she pronounced with finality. "That school is raising false alarms."

Gossip about the incident in Mrs. Rupert's class spread throughout the seventh grade at Burlington Middle School. After a few days, during a break in gym class, a few kids asked him to repeat the experiment for them. They would place their palm against his chest, and Eric would obligingly stop his heart for a few seconds. The kids giggled, thinking this was fun, and tried to duplicate Eric's feat. They couldn't. They wanted to know the trick.

Eric explained that there was no trick, at least not that he was aware of. He just willed it and it happened. The impromptu experiments continued in the cafeteria and on the basketball court after school. Eric and his friends tried to be discreet – mindful of the upset that had been caused in Mrs. Rupert's class.

Two days later, interest at the school had subsided. Among the twelve-year-olds at Burlington, gossip was transitory – their attention was now focused on a rumor that Mr. Martin was seen eating raw fish for lunch. (Mr. Martin's Japanese wife sent sushi with him in his lunch bag each day.) The story became successively exaggerated until some kids were reporting to their parents that Mr. Martin was a cannibal. Eric's day of brief fame was forgotten.

I heard a little of the neighborhood gossip about Eric and became curious. Wednesday evening, I went to Eric's room and closed the door behind me.

"I've heard two different kids say that you can make your heart stop."

Eric looked defiant. "I already told Dad that it was Mrs. Rupert's lousy equipment, not my heart."

I knew my brother well enough to see that he was lying. "So, it's true? You really can stop your heart?"

Eric was cornered. He nodded silently.

"Then let's see it." I sat on the floor in front of Eric and held his wrist, touching his artery with my thumb. His pulse was strong.

"How long do you want me to stop it for?" Eric asked.

I hesitated, unsure of what kind of trouble I was about to create. "Just stop it for a few seconds."

As I held his wrist, I watched him become completely unconscious for five seconds. I was so flustered that I forgot to hold onto his wrist, and never knew whether his heart had stopped or not. But I saw that something had happened — something abnormal.

"Don't do it anymore," I intoned, using my most authoritative big-brother tone. "Mom wouldn't like it."

Eric nodded and hung his head.

"And by the way, why did you lie to Dad when he asked you about Mrs. Rupert's class on Tuesday?"

"Because he wouldn't have understood."

"What's to understand? You stopped your heart! It's probably some kind of birth defect. Maybe you need surgery!"

At that moment, I recall being terrified for Eric. After all, he was playing with life and death! At the very least, we were fortunate that up until now, Eric hadn't been taken away from us by some scary government agent. My imagination went wild as I visualized Eric being held in some research building, poked and prodded by doctors from all over the world. But Eric looked contrite and with a caress on his back, I let the matter drop.

And that might have been the end of the whole story if not for Liam Sanders. In February, Liam brought his father's stethoscope to our house. Liam was in Mrs. Rupert's class when it all started. He had related the whole story to his family at dinner that same evening; his father dismissed the story as nonsense.

"Eric's not stopping his heart. He's merely slowing it down to the point that it's hard to detect," Dr. Sanders said.

After dinner, Dr. Sanders fished out an old stethoscope from a desk drawer in his study.

"This is the stethoscope they gave me in medical school," he told his son. "You'll be able to easily hear his heart with this." He showed Liam how to position the stethoscope and they practiced on each other.

Liam forgot to bring the stethoscope to Eric's clubhouse the next day, but on Thursday he pulled it from his pocket and told everyone about his Dad's verdict. Eric, mindful of the warning that I had issued the night before, called me down to the basement and asked my permission.

I was conflicted. I wasn't sure what had happened in my room the night before, but it struck me as dangerous when it happened.

But Dr. Sanders had told Liam it was safe, so who was I to object? At least with Liam's stethoscope, we could discover the truth. So, I sat on the floor with the other kids in the clubhouse, and told Eric and Liam to proceed.

Eric stopped his heart for two very long minutes. No one could detect a pulse, not even Liam Sanders with his dad's stethoscope. Unfortunately, as Liam was hunched over Eric's body, listening intently for signs of a heartbeat, Mom walked in. It was three-fifteen in the afternoon. She had come home from work at three, and had just changed from her nurse's uniform into jeans and a sweat shirt.

Mom came down the basement steps, carrying a plate of peanut butter cookies for Eric and his friends. She was surprised to see me downstairs, and more surprised by the kids huddled around Eric. As she approached Eric, the kids stepped aside. Mom's face turned pale. She touched the cold skin on Eric's face and panicked. She listened for his breath, grabbed both his wrists, and desperately tried to feel a pulse.

I tried to explain how it happened, but Mom didn't hear a word. She told me to call 911 as she stretched Eric out on the floor and started CPR. As soon as she pressed on his chest, Eric's eyelids fluttered and he awoke. Mom held Eric in her arms and wept. Liam Sanders and the other kids quickly left our house; I sat down next to Eric and began rubbing his cold feet.

Mom was deeply shaken. She had discounted the story about Mrs. Rupert's class, but this time she had seen it with her own eyes. Over the next four months, she took Eric to three different doctors. Dr. Sanders ran an EKG on Eric and pronounced him completely normal. Dr. Williams did a treadmill test and also gave him a clean bill of health. Dr. Burns, the chief of cardiology at St Luke's, shot radioactive goop into Eric's vein and watched it illuminate an x-ray machine. "Go ahead, Eric. Let's see you stop your heart," he said.

Eric readily complied, going into cardiac arrest for one full minute. Dr. Burns had charged the defibrillator and was a second away from giving Eric 1,000 volts. He looked very relieved when Eric's heart began beating spontaneously on its own.

Dr. Burns recommended that no further tests be run on Eric. "He proved he can stop his heart. We may never know how he does it, but it's damaging to his health and he must stop." He and Mom talked to Eric, explained the risks to him, and got Eric to promise to 'cease and desist.' I was immensely relieved that Dr. Burns didn't call in a squad of government agents to take my brother away.

After that, when kids at school asked Eric to stop his heart, he told them that he had lost the knack for it. And during the following months, the whole episode was largely forgotten.

My mind, in particular, was on other things. I was now a busy senior in high school. I was trying out for the rowing team, working on the yearbook staff, and practicing for my second attempt at the SAT's. I had scored 1256 on my first try and knew I could do better. Eric still held court with his friends in our basement every afternoon. At first, Mom made frequent, unannounced visits to Eric's clubhouse, as if she might find Eric unconscious again. But Eric was a model of good behavior. He completed his homework early every night before anyone asked. He was dressed for school before Mom came upstairs to wake him. He was quieter than before, but I was too busy to do more than notice.

Late one night in February 1991, I awoke to use the bathroom. As I walked in bare feet down the hallway, I could see light under Eric's bedroom door. I cracked open the door, peeked in, and saw him sitting motionless on the floor. His eyes were open, but glazed over. I hurried in and felt his head – ice cold. My own heart raced. I started to holler for Mom, but thought better of it. I didn't want to see her panic again. So, I sat on the floor facing Eric, grabbed his hands in mine, and whispered intently, "Come back, come back!" After another twenty seconds Eric abruptly shook his head and gasped for air.

As his eyes regained their focus, he looked at me sharply. "What are you doing in my room, Sam?"

"Eric, you promised Mom you wouldn't do this anymore!"

He rubbed his hands and looked at the floor. Annoyance had changed to repentance.

"Sam, you don't understand. This is something I have to do." He leaned back against his bed, eyes still on the floor. "There's something I never told you, Sam. I *see* things when I die - see, feel, and hear things. I didn't at first – at first, restarting my heart was like waking up from a deep sleep. But later, I remembered things that happened while I was dead – like dreams, but more real than dreams. I didn't want to upset Mom, but I needed to know where I went when my heart stopped."

Journal note to Dr. Sheila:

> *You made a comment that the voluntary stopping and starting of a human heart is a medical impossibility. Maybe so, but there are many precedents. Years after the incident in Mrs. Rupert's seventh-grade health class, I discovered detailed references in Buddhist and Hindu texts to 'Nirodha', a rare meditative state reached by spiritual masters. It is characterized by the cessation of body functions including breath and heartbeat. During the time of the last Buddha, certain ascetics would enter Nirodha for days at a time, returning with no ill effects. Some Buddhist scholars*

believe that Nirodha differs from actual death by the continuance of imperceptibly slight cardiac and respiratory functioning. Others believe Nirodha is nothing less than a miracle – a genuine death and subsequent resurrection.

Chapter 5
A Gentleman Named U Bo Thet

Our birth is but a sleep and a forgetting:
The soul that rises with us, our life's star
Hath had elsewhere its setting,
And cometh from afar...

from *"Ode: Intimations of Immortality from collections of Early Childhood"* by William Wordsworth

Away from our parents' earshot, Eric and I argued for days. He was obstinate.

"It's my body, and it's my life," he insisted. "No one can stop me."

I anguished and eventually gave in. He had now been stopping his heart almost every day for six months. If there were any ill effects, they should have appeared by now. How could I forbid something that appeared harmless? Besides, I really was intrigued. What were these experiences that he was having? Were they just the product of a child's vivid imagination, or something more? So, I agreed not to blow the whistle on my little brother – with one condition.

"From now on, you don't do it alone. I've got to be there."

"Agreed," Eric responded, somewhat reluctantly.

For three months, Eric and I charted the strange world that lay beyond his own life. Four or five nights per week, he would sit cross-legged on the floor, close his eyes, take a few deep breaths, and die for three minutes. I would sit on the floor with my legs outstretched, facing him. I was always anxious during the time he was gone, constantly checking the time on my watch. I had no idea what I would do if three minutes passed and he didn't return. If that happened, how could I ever explain it to Mom and Dad? They would surely blame me. I was five years older and should know better.

So, every night was a tug-of-war between my own misgivings and my desire to collect more information from Eric. The three minutes that he was gone seemed interminable. I would recheck my watch, convinced that I read it wrong. When he finally returned with a lurch and a gasp for air, I would rub his feet while he briskly rubbed his hands together. Once he was warm, he would tell me what had happened.

I figured the stories were only dreams, but they were fascinating because they were detailed, consistent, and progressive. Eric provided a detailed chronicle about the thoughts, feelings, and activities of a man in Rangoon, Burma during the 1960's.

Then I allowed myself to consider that these tales were more than dreams. For one thing, when I probed Eric for more details, he never hesitated in supplying them.

"U Bo Thet heard a commotion in the street a block away," Eric said.

I would ask "What was the name of the street?" or "Describe the man making the commotion," or "Were there any police present?"

The spontaneity and fluidity of the additional details

made me think Eric was tapping into something other than his own imagination.

But something else erased any lingering doubts. I had collected assorted street names, descriptions of buildings including large museums and hospitals, and names of minor officials in the Burmese government. With some assistance at the Santa Clara public library and an app called Old Maps Online, I was able to find an old street map of Rangoon, Burma, circa 1965. The map allowed me to verify the thirteen streets mentioned by Eric. I also found the three museums that U Bo Thet had visited. A little more searching in a Southeast Asia almanac identified the four government officials who were U Bo Thet's friends.

This probably wasn't enough proof to satisfy the standards of modern social science research. After all, Eric could have gone to the library just as I had, and could have perused the same online sources. But I knew Eric had not done that. This was enough evidence for me.

So, the stories were real. But real in what sense? Was Eric remembering a past life? Or was some other entity communicating to Eric? If so, what was its purpose?

Once I realized that these stories were anchored in reality, I began taking notes, filling a spiral notebook every week. I got Eric to fill in, as best as he could, everything I missed during the six months he was operating alone. I was spellbound. U Bo Thet was not a particularly important or powerful man. But his life was fascinating. Every day seemed full of human drama, humor, insight, and even mystery.

And as U Bo Thet's story unfolded, I became less anxious about the whole nightly process that Eric and I were engaged in. But I noticed that every time Eric used the 'D word' – 'I died', 'after I died', 'when I die' – my own heart would jump.

"Don't use that word!" I would snap.

"Why not? It's accurate."

"Maybe so, but it's also damn nerve-wracking. It reminds me of just how far out on a limb we've climbed. It reminds me how deeply we're violating the bounds of common sense."

"So, what word would you prefer?"

I thought about it for a moment.

"Trip! That's what we'll say. Don't tell me you died; tell me you took a trip."

Eric grinned. "This is silly, Sam. The word doesn't change what is happening. It's not a LSD trip."

"It changes the way I *feel* about what's happening. Just humor me."

Eric agreed, and from that night on, we avoided death's name.

Eric told me that a few seconds after stopping his heart, he would see a constellation of four brightly colored lights (blue, green, orange and yellow). The orange light burned the brightest. Without thinking, he would float toward the orange light – when he entered it, he felt enveloped in warmth. Then, a second later, he would find himself in another world, looking out through the eyes of this Burmese gentleman named U Bo Thet.

On Eric's first trip, U Bo Thet was in a small sunlit house with five others. U Bo Thet was talking to a slight woman with piercing black eyes, shiny black hair gathered tightly in a ponytail, and a mouth that was set in determination. Eric knew instinctively that this was U Bo Thet's wife, Nee. All the conversation was in Burmese, and the only words Eric understood were the occasional English expressions (e.g.

"President Kennedy," "atom bomb"). On his second contact with U Bo Thet, Eric spotted U Bo Thet's English desk calendar. It was turned to March 3, 1961.

During the first month (when Eric was tripping alone), he began to understand more of the Burmese language conversations. He didn't study it - he just seemed to assimilate it. By the middle of the second month, he understood all that was said.

After I had joined him in the sixth month, I gave him a quick language test.

"Say 'How are you?' in Burmese."

Eric met the question with a blank stare that lasted several seconds.

"Kaun bad hala?...it took me a while to recall."

After that, Eric became quite adept at recalling. He became fluent in Burmese, and also began inheriting U Bo Thet's knowledge of medicine, history, art and music.

I learned that U Bo Thet was a dedicated Buddhist. He was also a doctor who practiced primary care from a small clinic in his home. When he wasn't treating patients, he played the violin, visited with relatives, took long walks in the city parks, and read books in three languages. And on Monday, Wednesday, and Friday evenings he taught Buddhist meditation to a class of lay people. The meditation classes were the most important part of his life — more important than the practice of medicine. U Bo Thet had a favorite maxim: "Medicine can cure the ills of this present life, but meditation can cure the ills of all our lives; past, present, and future."

Burma was a Buddhist country. And in Burma, meditation was not just for monks. Men, women, and children from all parts of society would gather for meditation. Burmese families often spent their vacations on extended meditation retreats. Many of the meditation teachers were monks. But some, like U Bo Thet, were lay teachers. In Rangoon, people spoke of U Bo Thet with the same admiration as the most accomplished monks, the Sayadaws.

Classes took place in a garage on U Bo Thet's property that had been converted into a meditation hall. A small shrine at the front held a large painting of the Buddha as he delivered his first sermon 'The Setting in Motion of the Wheel of the Dharma.' On either side of the magnificent painting was a vase of fresh flowers. A spotless hardwood floor was lined by neat rows of meditation cushions. U Bo Thet's meditation hall could accommodate thirty students, but it wasn't big enough. U Bo Thet would leave the entrance door open so overflow students could sit on the porch and still hear him talk.

Students were not charged for participating in U Bo Thet's meditation course. He said the Dharma – the Buddha's teachings – must be free to all who request it. He did accept dana, or gifts, to defray the expense of keeping fresh flowers in the hall.

It was clear that the duration of Eric's trip of three minutes or less did not correspond to time in U Bo Thet's world. Eric would experience an entire day in U Bo Thet's life during one trip. Eric tried to stay with U Bo Thet as he drifted off to sleep at night, but it never worked. As soon as U Bo Thet slept, Eric was returned.

And although Eric's trips moved progressively forward in U Bo Thet's life, they were discontinuous. One week's worth of trips from our room in Santa Clara corresponded to about 10 weeks in U Bo Thet's world. So, Eric missed a lot. His first task on each trip became catching up. On March 12,

1963, a very emotional U Bo Thet had delivered the eulogy at the funeral of his one Western student, Daniel West, who had died in an automobile accident. Eric had become as fond of West as U Bo Thet. And Eric was present the day of West's death, grieving with U Bo Thet at the news. But when Eric tripped the following night, he found he had already missed the funeral. He could remember the emotional eulogy that U Bo Thet had offered, but regretted that he didn't share in the experience directly.

Gradually Eric learned to accept the gaps. He became able to absorb U Bo Thet's memories of the lapsed days and merge quickly into U Bo Thet's ongoing life. As the months passed in our world, U Bo Thet was aging in years. A glance at U Bo Thet's calendar or the daily paper confirmed this. During the ten months that Eric made contact with him, U Bo Thet aged eleven years.

Eric's personality started to change as he incorporated more of U Bo Thet's thoughts and memories into his own consciousness. He was still my little brother in that scrawny thirteen-year-old body, but he was also an accomplished Burmese physician. I wasn't always sure who I was talking to. For me it didn't really matter, but I cautioned Eric.

"Be careful what you say to Mom and Dad. You have to remember —in their eyes you're still supposed to be a normal adolescent, with all the naiveté that goes with adolescence. So, don't start expounding on Buddhist scripture or medical ethics – they will know something is awry, and they will want an explanation."

Eric tried his best, but it was hard to consistently play a false role. Sometimes he revealed too much when Mom or Dad was listening. In the summer of 1992, while Eric and I were on vacation from school, we would meet Mom for lunch at St. Luke's hospital cafeteria. On this particular day, Mom told us about a patient in intensive care. She was worried about him. She described his symptoms, his blood test results, and the doctor's suspicion that he had encephalitis. I could see Eric squirm. He couldn't stop himself from interjecting - "Has he been abroad?"

Mom's eyebrow rose as she looked at Eric. "As a matter of fact, the doctor thinks he contracted the virus in Bangkok – he was there ten days ago."

Eric muttered to himself as he chewed a mouthful of tuna sandwich. Mom asked him to repeat himself. Eric was trapped. I wanted desperately for him to say nothing, to change the subject, to knock his glass of soda onto the floor – anything but tip Mom off to everything we had been doing in his room for the last year.

"Dengue," said Eric. "Sounds more like dengue fever than encephalitis. The plasma drop is characteristic of dengue, but not encephalitis." Eric saw the surprise on Mom's face and started backpedaling.

"It's just a guess, Mom. I wrote a school essay on epidemics for Mr. Bradford's Geography class. It covered encephalitis and dengue. It's all just a big coincidence." Eric paused, smiled, and said with a shrug, "Wouldn't it be wild if I was right?"

Of course he was right. After we finished lunch, Mom asked the attending physician in intensive care if the patient might have dengue. The doctor seemed intrigued by the question, checked his Merck Manual, called a colleague, and confirmed the new diagnosis. The patient's medication was changed, and he was discharged 48 hours later.

But this episode wasn't over. When she got home, Mom asked to see Eric's essay. Eric said he left it in his locker at school. That lie gave him enough time to create the missing essay. Mom read it, shrugged her shoulders, and handed it back to Eric. She must have thought Eric's story was plausible, even if a bit improbable. During the next week, she made a disconcerting habit of opening the door to Eric's room without knocking. We decided to postpone his trips until she stopped checking on us.

The hiatus in Eric's trips gave me time to sift through the implications of all that had happened.

Was Eric just a passive observer, watching a period of history replayed as in a movie theater? Or was he an active participant, able to influence what U Bo Thet said and did? If he was a participant, did that mean that Eric could change history?

I asked Eric. On Sunday afternoon, after our parents had left to go grocery shopping. I asked the question solemnly – aware that it might be the most important question ever posed. "Eric, did you ever make U Bo Thet do something that he didn't choose himself?"

Eric barely looked up from the funny papers he had spread across the living room floor. "Sure, but why is that important?"

I started to explain why it was not only important, but why his answer had just rocked the foundations of Western philosophy and science, but I stopped myself. Eric was a brilliant kid. He had absorbed everything that U Bo Thet had learned in 60 years of life. But Eric was also just a 12-year-old kid, and he didn't yet appreciate the significance of it all. This wasn't the time. I shrugged my shoulders, sat on the floor next to him, and grabbed a section of funnies.

After a minute, Eric resumed the conversation. "I'll tell you about the most vivid example of my steering U Bo Thet's actions. One afternoon in 1972, U Bo Thet was sitting at his desk composing letters. I wanted him to write a letter to Dad. It was a struggle. I kept whispering to him. He would pause, look a bit puzzled, and then ignore me. But I persisted. And finally, I felt him yield. He pulled out a fresh piece of writing paper, picked up his pen, and wrote 'Dear Mr. Hill.' I guided him through the whole process including addressing an envelope and depositing it in the mailbox."

My interest was riveted. "And so – what happened? Was the letter delivered?"

"I'm not sure. I wanted to ask Dad if he had gotten an unexpected letter back in 1972, but I wasn't sure how to ask without opening a big can of worms."

I resolved then that, somehow, I was going to find that letter. If it existed, it would be the paradox of all time.

Chapter 6
Taking the Untraveled Road

If one advances confidently in the direction of his dreams,
and endeavors to live the life which he has imagined...
From *Walden,* by Henry David Thoreau

When I turned eighteen, my parents gave me a used 1984 Volkswagen Beetle – it was bright lemon yellow. I preferred 'sunshine yellow,' but Eric called it my lemon. Except for the color, it was exactly what I had wanted. (Of course, I learned long ago that my parents loved me whether or not I got what I wanted for birthdays.) In the 1980's, college campuses and high school parking lots were full of beetles. They got over 30 miles to the gallon, had great traction because of the rear engine, didn't need antifreeze, and were easy to fix. A used Volkswagen like mine cost less than $3,000.

The day we got it, I took the whole family out for ice cream. Dad rode up front with me; Eric and Mom in the back seat. It was only eight blocks to the Dairy Queen, and we were back at our house in less than an hour. Yet that hour feels frozen in time. I remember everything that was said. I remember the expression on my mother's face. I can still see Eric as he looked in my rearview mirror that day.

For an eighteen-year-old boy, a car is freedom – as I lovingly waxed it, I fantasized about the incredible trips I would take in her. There was no good reason, I thought, why Eric and I couldn't hop in one day and drive to New York. Or Fairbanks, Alaska. Or Cape Horn. They were all connected by land, and even if the roads were bad, my Beetle would get us there. A car is freedom – and possibility.

63

Three days after my birthday, I had to make a difficult decision. I had applied to two colleges – UCLA and Wickham. Wickham was less than a mile from our home in Santa Clara. It was a Jesuit College, with a great basketball team, and a strong liberal arts program. The departments of Religion and Philosophy were well-regarded, and that's what I wanted to study. Tuition was steep but I could live at home and avoid room and board charges.

The problem was that I got accepted to both UCLA and Wickham. UCLA had no allure for me. It was three hundred miles away. I would not be permitted to take my beloved Beetle with me until sophomore year. It was ten times bigger than Wickham, and I wouldn't know anyone there. The only reason I applied is because Mom handed me the application and watched over my shoulder while I filled it out. When I finished, I looked up and she had tears in her eyes.

"My four years at UCLA were the best of my life," she said. "I pledged Alpha Tau Delta, the nursing sorority. Twenty-five years later, I am still close to every one of my sorority sisters." Her voice cracked as she talked, and she dabbed at her eyes with a Kleenex. "I would be so proud if you went there."

"Your Mom's right!" Dad had been eavesdropping from the kitchen. "Everything important that I ever learned – was during my four years at the University of Idaho – I learned to love history, girls, and cars; not necessarily in that order. Living in Los Angeles for four years will give you a sense of independence and autonomy that will serve you the rest of your life."

I didn't like the way this conversation was going. I made my stand.

"I don't want to be independent. I like living here. I like Santa Clara. I like our church, my friends from school; I like the park, the fishing hole, the Dairy Queen. I like climbing the old poplar tree in our back yard. And these things are not relics of childhood that have to be abandoned. For me, they're happiness. Why should I give up happiness just because I've turned eighteen?"

I heard clapping. Eric was in the doorway giving me an ovation. "Bravo, Sam!"

Then he saw the disappointment on Mom's face. He paused and shifted gears, addressing Mom and Dad.

"Look folks – Sam is at a crossroad. He has to choose between knowledge and wisdom. He can get knowledge at either school. He'll learn about science and philosophy and religion at either school. But where is he going to find wisdom? Where must he go to discern the purpose of his life? To find the builder of this house we call heaven and earth? Sam wants to find the housebuilder, and he's got to take the right road."

"What the devil are you talking about, Eric?" my father snapped. "I think your mother and I know a little more about this than you."

Eric smiled, turned, and headed outside to play with his friends.

But his speech had emboldened me. "I'm not sure I understand what Eric said either. But I think he's right. I'm searching for something bigger than a bunch of college courses. And I'm going to find it here in Santa Clara, at Wickham College."

During May, U Bo Thet began to die. In U Bo Thet's world, it was January 1977. U Bo Thet's world now lagged only fourteen years behind ours. In fact, it occurred to me that I was now living in both worlds. I was seventeen in this world, and three in U Bo Thet's. In principle, there was no reason why Eric couldn't pick up the phone when he was tripping, make a long-distance call, and talk to his three-year-old brother, Sam. But we wouldn't have the chance for any such experiments. On May 18, 1991 Eric aborted his trip. He returned with tears in his eyes. He had seen only four lights – the orange light was gone. U Bo Thet was dead in both worlds.

The next day, Eric and I went to the public library and searched the obituaries in the *Asian Times*, a weekly newspaper and the only Asian source in the library that included obituaries. In the March 6th edition was a one-inch square announcement that the famous Burmese meditation master and physician, Sayagi U Bo Thet, had died from pancreatic cancer on February 28, 1977. He was survived by his wife Nee, and a brother, U Chi Tan. Above the announcement was a grainy photograph of U Bo Thet, taken when he was fifty-two.

Eric said he wanted to stop tripping for a few months out of respect for U Bo Thet. There were still four lights to explore, and the blue one now burned brightest.

"When the time is right, I'll see who lives inside the blue light," Eric said. "But for now, I'm just going to enjoy my memories of U Bo Thet."

That September, I began my freshman year at Wickham. With every passing week, I became surer that I had made the right decision. I had it all. My favorite classes were *Introduction to Religious Beliefs* and *Foundations of Philosophical Thought*. They were survey courses to prepare students with concepts and thinking skills for later courses. We reviewed Christianity, Buddhism, Islam, and Hinduism. We studied

Aristotle, Locke, Hobbes, and Nietzsche. But all these scholars didn't help much in understanding what had happened to my brother.

I had sixteen spiral notebooks filled with notes from U Bo Thet's life, but wasn't sure what they meant. Was this reincarnation, as the Hindus understood reincarnation? If I could turn my spiral notebooks into a well-researched case study of an actual reincarnation, it would be a work that would stand next to the great works of history.

What if it wasn't reincarnation? Maybe it was really a form of time travel. That would be no less exciting. To bring time travel from the realm of science fiction to documented fact would be a staggering accomplishment.

Every day after classes I spent an hour at the library, leafing through books about psychic and near-death phenomena. I wanted to find other cases like Eric's. If there were others like Eric who had courted death and made the journey across space and time, at least some of their stories should be in the published literature. If I could find them, I could write the authors, establish dialogues, and maybe build a community of psychic researchers.

I found accounts from other people who had died and returned to tell about it in the genre of books about 'near death' experiences. Their reports bore some similarities to Eric's; they told of brightly colored lights and described feeling pulled towards one which burned brighter than the rest. But I found no accounts of occupying another's body and mind except in some science fiction stories. After an entire semester of afternoons in the Wickham library, I stopped looking. What I had collected in my spiral notebooks was unprecedented. I was on my own.

Chapter 7
Foreboding and Loss

*And then you think of a fellow who an hour before was
full of life and fun, and he's lying dead; it's all so cruel
and so meaningless. It's hard not to ask yourself what
life is all about and whether there's any sense to it or
whether it's all a tragic blunder of blind fate.*

From *The Razor's Edge* by W. Somerset Maugham

In January 1994, Eric was sixteen and in tenth grade. I
was finishing my junior year at Wickham. I spent my time
reading great works by great minds like Thomas Aquinas,
John Stuart Mill, and William Blake. And I couldn't wait for
the next day's classes; all my classes were now upper-level
and were conducted in small seminars. My professors used
the classic Socratic Method: Argument, Refutation, and
Counterargument. We never seemed to arrive at any fixed
truths, but it was fun trying. For the first time in my life, I
actually enjoyed doing homework.

Dad was happy that I was enjoying college, but skeptical
about my major. He would hold up the Sunday classified
ads and say, "I don't see anyone trying to hire philosophers."

But he saw how motivated I was. "Who knows?" my Dad
bellowed over the dinner table. "Maybe you'll get a Ph.D.
and become a professor."

I hadn't thought about it before, but maybe getting a
Ph.D. would be a good idea. Maybe all those spiral notebooks could become a doctoral dissertation. I smiled at my
father and said, "When everybody else calls me Doctor Hill,
you can still call me Sam."

The last weekend of January, Mom and Dad drove to Idaho Falls to visit Dad's sister, Ruth. Dad's mother and father died in 1970 and 1973 respectively, and Ruth was Dad's only blood relative. In the summer, Ruth would take the bus to Santa Clara and spend a week with us. In the winter, we would drive to Idaho to see her.

But Dad and Ruth were closer than their semiannual visits would suggest. They exchanged letters every week. I remember seeing Dad as he sat at his big roll top desk, finishing a three-page letter to Ruth and folding family snapshots into it before he stuffed it into a large brown envelope. "Why not just talk to Aunt Ruth on the phone?" I asked.

"I want to tell her how I feel." He swiveled his chair to face me. "Sometimes it's easier to be honest in writing."

The honest truth about my Dad. He graduated from Idaho Falls High School in 1960 and tried to enlist in the Army. Since his glasses looked like the bottoms of coke bottles, poor eyesight kept him out – and he enrolled that fall in the University of Idaho. With a Magna Cum Laude in Business earned in 1964, he landed his first job as a salesman with Aetna Insurance. He was on a business trip to California in the summer of 1969 when he met a young nurse named Jane Tyler. He married Mom a month later, and moved into her home in Santa Clara.

His sister, Ruth, never left Idaho Falls. She worked as a secretary in City Hall, and when she was twenty-five, she married Mayor Rufus Biggs, who was twenty years her senior. Rufus was hard-working until the day he died – which happened soon after he shoveled three feet of snow from his driveway in the winter of 1992. At Rufus' funeral, Dad asked Ruth to move to Santa Clara and share our home. Ruth politely declined, pointing to the rows of close friends that filled the chapel of St. Gregory's Church. "I could never leave all my friends."

Dad kept close by writing and making a trip to Idaho every winter. I loved making the trip with him. Eric and I would sit in the back seat and pass the time playing 'Twenty Questions,' 'Ghost,' and 'Gin Rummy.' When we got tired of that, we'd crank up the radio to a 1960's Oldies station if we could find it. Eric and I knew the words to most of the top forty tunes of the decade and our voices would drown out the radio as we sang along.

The winter of 1994 was the first time Eric and I didn't go. Mom and Dad had not been able to schedule their visit over the Christmas holidays, and they didn't want to take us out of school. They also figured that at seventeen, I was old enough to take care of Eric and the house for a week.

They left on Friday morning while Eric and I were at school. The next day, Eric and I feasted on pizza delivered hot to our door. We were energized. It was the first time we had been left alone in the house overnight. We stayed up late the night before, and spent Saturday eating everything that Mom would have disapproved of. We even delved into Dad's liquor cabinet to taste his brandy and it tasted awful. When our festivities hit a lull, Eric asked me to watch him while he tripped. Not needing the usual secrecy, we used the living room floor. Eric sat up straight, closed his eyes, and became very still. A minute later his heart and his breathing stopped. He was off on a journey, presumably with U Bo Thet, and I opened my journal, ready to take notes when he came back.

But this evening Eric's trip was cut short. After just a few seconds, Eric's body began trembling and he lurched back to life with fright in his eyes.

"It's Mom and Dad!" Eric had to wrestle the words from his throat. "They're dead."

I dropped my journal, grabbed the phone and called Aunt Ruth. She answered after seven rings, sobbing "God, no! GOD, NO!" The police were at her house, and had given up trying to take a statement from her. Mom and Dad had left an hour earlier for a movie and had collided with a drunk driver. They died instantly.

The funeral for Mom and Dad was held at McCormick's Funeral Home in Santa Clara, where all of our extended family members and about forty friends gathered. I tried to give a eulogy at the front of the chapel, but kept choking up. I finally sat down and yielded the lectern to Eric.

I knew Eric had been up all night writing his eulogy, but I had not read it. I did save it though – here it is:

> *How can I honor the memory of my parents? My first inclination was to tell you all the good things I remember about them. Like when my father took us camping when I was nine. Or when my mother hired a clown for my tenth birthday. But I don't think memories suffice. We should honor our parents for the things we don't remember.*
>
> *Try an experiment with me. Everyone, close your eyes and draw your attention to a point within your bodies. Feel your breath as it enters your nostrils, and as it leaves. Now imagine your mother, as she is nine months pregnant with you. She has endured months of pain and discomfort, morning sickness, back aches, sore legs. But she's endured it all with a sense of joy – she knows you're on your way and she can't wait to see you. Your father, too, is anxiously awaiting your*

arrival – he's been encouraging your mother, taking on extra chores so she can rest.

Imagine it's the day of your birth. Your mother is feeling excruciating pain as she struggles with labor, but her tears erupt from both joy and pain. As she struggles, she thinks lovingly of you. When you emerge from her womb, you are covered with blood and mucous and are bawling loudly. Your mother doesn't care – she is swept away by the miracle of your birth. She just wants to hold you, to whisper in your ear how much she cares. Your father is standing near, stroking your mother's hair. He has lost his battle to contain his tears, and his face is now wet with them.

For the rest of the day, you are the center of your parents' universe. All their thoughts, all their energy, are with you. You are completely helpless, completely vulnerable. You can't do anything for yourself – you don't know where you are, you can't even lift your head. And you don't have to – your mother and father see to your every need. When they get you home, their lives are transformed by you. They will awaken to your cries in the middle of the night and cradle you back to sleep. They will read you stories, show you off to relatives, and dream about what you will be when you grow up. Their love for you is so great; they would readily sacrifice their own lives for yours. They would give up anything; do anything, to ensure your safety and well-being.

Can you feel the intensity of your parents' love? Maybe you can't remember these things that happened at your birth, but you can feel them. Today I honor my parents, Robert and Jane, not just for the things I remember, but for the things I don't. When I needed them most, they were there. When I was helpless, they gave me everything.

When the memorial service ended, Eric and I had to endure a gauntlet of our parents' friends. It took an hour and a half before Edith Murphy, Dad's high school teacher, and the last one in line, offered me her sympathy and assured me that Mom and Dad were now in a better place. I really wasn't listening to her. My feet hurt from standing so long, my hand hurt from shaking so many hands, and I was relieved the service was over. I had stopped listening to the particular words people were saying at about the halfway point. Instead I sported a brave look on my face and nodded somberly.

Edith finally stepped forward to greet Eric, and I felt free at last. I had greeted ninety-three people and showed at least feigned interest in each of them. I retreated quickly toward an unoccupied chair. From there I watched Eric, who was now encountering Edith Murphy. Unlike me, Eric was shaking the ninety-third hand with genuine interest. Eric's eyes were riveted on Edith's as he listened intently to her words. Why wasn't I surprised by this? Because I had never seen Eric ignore anybody – not even the ninety-third well-wisher. Edith reiterated to Eric her firm belief that Mom and Dad were in paradise. Eric paused, squeezed her hand, and said, "I think they're really in Cincinnati, but I guess that's a lot like paradise." Edith appeared momentarily nonplussed, but she recovered with a giggle and a pat of her hand on Eric's cheek.

On the way home, I asked Eric why he had been glib

with Mrs. Murphy.

"I wasn't glib, Sam. Mom and Dad have been reborn. When I tripped last week, instead of gravitating automatically to the orange light, I felt drawn toward the azure one. It radiated an unusual energy, and I wanted to see the source. When I merged into the light, I found myself still disembodied and floating. But there was a city below. I could just see the skyline. And there was a strong sense of Mom and Dad's presence. Not calling me – I didn't feel they were summoning me; but they were somehow wordlessly announcing their presence. I was content with that; it seemed enough to know that their lives flowed on."

Eric paused and gazed out of the car window.

"But before I retreated and came back from the trip," Eric continued. "I realized that the city skyline was familiar. Instead of retreating I moved a bit closer and recognized Riverfront Stadium. It was a landmark that Dad and I had watched countless times on TV. Karma works just like that. Dad became a baseball fan after he met his first girlfriend, Melissa Charles, who was from Columbus, Ohio. She was a baseball fanatic and taught Dad, who had no previous interest in sports of any kind, to love the game as well."

Some of the stuff my little brother said was so profound. But this wasn't. Eric's story seemed to me nothing short of preposterous, and I let him know. "So, what are you saying, Eric? Should we drive to Cincinnati, pick them up, and bring them back home?" As soon as I spoke, I realized that my voice carried too much caustic sarcasm, and I blushed at my own insolence.

By this time in our lives, Eric was used to my occasional rants. He was not put out.

"No Sam." Eric replied. "They're infants, they're safe,

and each of them was born into a good family. As they grow up, they will probably have no memory of Robert and Jane Hill, or us, or Idaho, or Santa Clara. Although they might – I'm proof of that. But whether they remember or not, it's still them. The same two souls that gave us life endure today."

We didn't talk the rest of the way home. Instead, I began mentally reviewing the circumstances in which Eric and I had been left. Aunt Ruth wanted both of us to come to Idaho Falls and live with her. I had politely declined, and assured her that Eric and I would be alright where we were. I was twenty-one and by the terms of our parents' will, I was Eric's legal guardian. We had the house which Mom and Dad had paid off eight years earlier. Our parents also had some savings – only about $20,000 – but Dad also had a $1,000,000 life insurance policy. (He was an insurance salesman, after all.) Eric and I would soon have a check for the entire amount. I would be graduating from Wickham next year and I already had a job offer as an entry-level manager from the Santa Clara Post Office. The three summers that I had spent there as a management intern had paid off. They were offering me a starting salary at $36,450.

I didn't know how Mom and Dad were doing in Cincinnati, but I strangely felt that Eric and I would be fine.

Chapter 8
Just the Two of Us

What is a friend? One soul dwelling in two bodies.
From *Diogenes Laertius, Lives of Eminent Philosophers*
by Aristotle

In the months following the funeral, Eric and I gradually adjusted to life on our own. I learned to cook – a job that Mom had always claimed for herself. I showed Eric how to take over mowing – a job that I had always done – and he kept the lawn trimmed. He tended the garden as well. I knew nothing about gardening, but apparently U Bo Thet did, so Eric did too.

It took me three months before I felt comfortable disturbing the contents of Mom and Dad's room. There were many mornings when I would just stand in the bedroom doorway and gaze at the room, which was just as they had left it. Letters lay on the desk that Dad had just opened before leaving for Idaho. Mom's favorite bottle of cologne sat on her dresser with the cap off, and I could still detect its faint scent. They were still here, bits of them anyway; I couldn't bear destroying what was left.

By April 1994, I could go in and pick up the letters without feeling like I was violating sacred space. I put the cap back on Mom's cologne and carefully packed everything belonging to my parents into four large footlockers. I stacked them in the furthest corner of the basement. And on April 16, I began hanging my own clothes in their closet, putting my own letters and cologne on their dresser. That night I slept in their bed for the first time.

Of course, I was already running things long before I slept in their bed. I had to. First, I transferred my parents' bank accounts, stocks, bonds, and insurance benefits to a new account that Eric and I opened. Then I began tackling bills, taxes, thank you letters, grocery shopping, and car maintenance – the countless details that Mom and Dad had handled. Parents do a lot of stuff that kids are completely unaware of. And it's not enjoyable stuff; it's tedious and time consuming. Now I had to do it all. And attend college. And cook dinner.

But I have to give Eric credit. He jumped in and helped a lot. Eric had no interest in paperwork, but enjoyed working outdoors and with his hands. So, he tended the lawn and garden, did laundry, vacuuming, and ironing. I did the shopping, taxes, bills, and cooking. As we settled into a routine, I actually began to enjoy my newfound independence and responsibility. I began acting very paternal toward Eric, checking nightly to see if he needed help with his homework or advice about school.

He only tripped twice since Mom and Dad's death. His experience floating over Cincinnati had been healing for him, but he was still apprehensive about having another 'bad' trip. Eric's talk about bad trips reminded me of what people said about LSD in the sixties. Three months after the funeral, he asked "Should I abandon my trips? What's the use? It leads me places that I'm no longer sure I want to go."

I had expected this, but hadn't expected him to ask in this way. I thought he would ask for my permission to continue, not my assent that he stop. It caught me off guard, and I found myself arguing the opposite of what I had planned.

"Your ability to join with other beings in other times - it's not just an accident of nature, Eric. It *means* something. We haven't figured out why you have this gift and what it means, but I feel that there is a reason for it all. You should push ahead and find out."

For the next month, I wasn't sure what Eric had decided to do, and I didn't press him. If he was tripping, he was doing it in private and not discussing it with me. That situation might have continued for more months if I had not fallen down the stairs. I was carrying an armload of old magazines and couldn't see the steps below me. I misjudged the first step off the landing and tumbled hard down the final flight. I'm usually pretty stoical about pain, but this really hurt, and I cried out. I was barefoot and could see my ankle promptly swelling and turning various shades of purple. Eric was in the back yard but heard me cry and rushed in to help.

"Get some ice from the freezer!" I muttered between teeth clenched against the pain.

"I have a better idea," said Eric. He bounded up the steps and came back a few seconds later with a small silk purse, embroidered with Chinese dragons. He unfolded the purse, revealing a set of acupuncture needles.

"Where did you get those?" I asked.

Eric smiled. "I ordered them from Burma. From the same store in Rangoon where U Bo Thet got his medical supplies. The store is still in business. I wrote them two months ago and told them I was an American doctor and an old friend of U Bo Thet's. They still revere U Bo Thet over there. They always send me whatever I ask for." As he talked, he positioned me on my back on the floor and rolled up my pants leg. He took an alcohol swab and cleaned two spots on either side of my knee and quickly inserted needles. Then another needle in my right ear. And another in between the thumb and forefinger of my right hand. He slowly twisted the last needle back and forth.

"Close your eyes and breathe," said Eric. As I did, I drifted into a dreamlike trance. Eric continued to talk, but his voice sounded like it was coming from miles away. After what seemed like a few seconds, I opened my eyes and sat up. Eric had folded up his acupuncture purse and was sitting in a chair across the room.

"So, how's your ankle now?" he asked.

I looked at it. There was no sign of the injury; no swelling; no discoloration; no pain. I stood up on it to test it. Good as new! "It was bright purple just a few seconds ago! How did you do it?" I asked.

"Not a few seconds. You've been out for an hour." I glanced at the clock. Eric was right – more than an hour had passed, yet it seemed like seconds. I sat back down on the stairs and looked expectantly at Eric.

"U Bo Thet was not only trained in western medicine, he was a master of traditional Chinese medicine. Through repeated trips, I absorbed a great deal of his medical knowledge. Eventually, it made me restless. What's the point of knowing all this stuff if I don't use it? But I don't have the credentials that U Bo Thet had. He was first in his graduating class at Rangoon Medical School. Even though I have inherited U Bo Thet's knowledge, I haven't inherited his credentials. My options are limited. Acupuncture, Chinese herbs, Qi Jong; they're not viewed as 'real medicine' here in the West. So, I figured I could practice these ancient healing arts without a problem. I've treated a dozen or so friends from school and from church. I even treated Bobby Sanders' Labrador Retriever. The dog is fourteen and has bad arthritis ... that is, *had* bad arthritis. She's pretty frisky now."

I continued rubbing my ankle. My ankle was feeling

fine, but I wasn't. I didn't like the feeling of being excluded from Eric's life. I was his older brother. I should have been informed. I took a breath before I spoke. I didn't want to come across as ungrateful or overly critical.

"Eric, you need to keep me better informed. I need to know what you're up to. Until you turn eighteen, remember, I'm in charge." As soon as I said that, I felt a little ashamed – after all, he had probably just rescued me from what would have been two weeks of recuperation on crutches. "But thanks, Eric, for your help. My ankle feels fine." Eric nodded slightly and headed back to his chores in the yard.

The acupuncture was wonderful. I kept leaning on my ankle, turning it, twisting it, thinking that the pain would start up again. It still seemed too good to be true.

Chapter 9
Our Home and Our Town

He is happiest, be he king or peasant,
who finds peace in his home.
By Johann Wolfgang Von Goethe

Eric and I gradually adapted to the loss of our parents. We had some vital supports to help us with the transition – our home and our town. As much as I missed Mom and Dad, I also felt immensely grateful for the house we lived in, and for the town of Santa Clara. Of course, I didn't have much to compare it with. I had only traveled a little – to Idaho, Los Angeles, and San Francisco. But I had read extensively about other towns and other lands. Eric and I were blessed. Every morning that I awoke in the large Victorian home at the end of Blackbird Court in Santa Clara, California, I felt like I belonged – in this house, in this town. It was a priceless feeling, the feeling that my life belonged to something bigger than myself. It's why now, many years later, I still awaken in exactly the same place.

The feeling is not so intense today. Now I frequently grasp for half-remembered images of old Santa Clara. Today Santa Clara bustles; it is the center of Silicon Valley and high technology. But a few short decades ago, it was a picturesque old mission village with the "old quad" anchoring the center of town, bordered by Central Park on the east, and Wickham College on the west. Central Park was the home to the Triton Museum and gardens, as well as a twelve-acre lake. It was the perfect place to stroll on Sundays and feed the pigeons. The town was compact enough to encourage walking. I rode my bike to classes at Wickham, just a mile away. It was a ten-minute ride, including stop lights, and bike racks were plentiful on campus – certainly more plentiful than parking spaces, which were scarce even then. Eric walked fifteen minutes each way to his high school. Mom and Dad's van spent most of the time parked in our driveway. When Eric and I would use it on Saturday mornings for our trip to the stores, it would protest its lack of use by refusing to start for several seconds. It worked more agreeably after Eric and I began driving it to church on Sundays.

Eric and I still attended St. Mary's Episcopal Church and it wasn't because of faith. I think at that time, Eric and I had more faith in Buddhism than the Episcopal Church canon. I had filled several volumes with U Bo Thet's wise counsel on Buddhist theory and practice. Frankly, it was more compelling than anything I learned in Sunday School at St. Mary's.

But St. Mary's was home. It was where our parents belonged, and it was where Eric and I had been coming every Sunday for as long as we could remember. We came because we still felt connected to the people, Father John, and the sanctuary with its beautiful stained-glass windows.

Of course, our real home was the three-story white Victorian that our parents had left us – the house on Blackbird Court where we grew up. Blackbird Court is a short, dead-end street with three homes on each side. Ours is the last one on the right, the one with the small marble fountain in front and the woods behind. All six homes were built by Sanders Brothers in 1952, and although not identical, all six were built in the same Victorian style – steep gabled roofs, corniced eaves, angled bay windows and Corinthian-columned porches. The front of each home featured a turret with faceted glass windows. Max Sanders was inspired by the Charles Copeland Morse Mansion on Fremont Street. Although the six houses on Blackbird Court didn't approach the grandeur of the 5500 square foot Morse Mansion, they projected much of its classic Victorian style. The interior of each was deliberately partitioned into small functional areas – a parlor, a formal dining room, a galley kitchen, and five small bedrooms suitable for a large family. The home builder lined the outside street with new elm trees. Over the years, the elms have grown to towering heights, cloaking both the street and the six homes from sun and wind. An old Chinese proverb says, 'One generation plants the trees; another gets the shade.'

Our stately home, our historic church, and the dozens of townspeople who had known Eric and me since our births; they were the roots that held us close to Santa Clara. Wickham College, from which I would soon be graduating, was the other jewel of the town. Although lacking a national reputation, it was the kind of small liberal arts school that still valued the great books, small classes, and elderly professors in tweed jackets that taught ancient Greek literature. It was the ideal place for me. And I hoped it would be the place for Eric.

Of course, Eric was getting the world's most unusual education. He was being mentored by one of the great intellectuals of the Far East, the Burmese physician and meditation master U Bo Thet. U Bo Thet was dead, and didn't know he was mentoring Eric, but the process was still active. By the time Eric turned sixteen, there was little in U Bo Thet's expansive knowledge that Eric had not absorbed. Watching Jeopardy on television with Eric became annoying – he rattled off answers to categories in literature, art, music, and science without hesitation.

Eric was learning the easy way – just recalling what he already knew in past lives. And I was learning the hard way – laboring page by page through the great books. I wonder how many of these books I had already learned, in another place and time. I guess most of us spend our lives relearning what we can't remember. And then the cycle begins again. Eric's way seemed so much more *efficient*. He could quickly assimilate all the wisdom of several past lives and move on from there. He learned Burmese the easy way – he was now nearly fluent, and had never cracked a book. He had to learn French the hard way – taking French I and II in high school. He barely squeaked by. I think he may have hoped that if he kept tripping, he would stumble across a French-speaking karmic ancestor. That didn't work, and he reluctantly sat down to the monotonous vocabulary drills that the rest of us endure.

Given that U Bo Thet was a physician, I figured Eric Hill could easily complete the pre-med curriculum at Wickham and go on to medical school. My mother, a nurse, always hoped one of us would become a doctor. The medical profession conveys high status and I thought if I steered Eric in the right direction, he could achieve Mom's hope.

But it was not to be. Eric was a lot of things, but he was not a seeker of social status. At the beginning of tenth grade, Eric told me he wasn't going to college. "It would not be an efficient use of my time," he said. "I've got other ideas that I want to pursue, and I don't want to be sidetracked by college."

"Is that what you think I've been doing for three years at Wickham? Going down a sidetrack?" I spoke with a sneer, immediately aware of my own defensiveness.

"No, Sam. Wickham is the right place for you. You are

doing wonderfully there. You'll look back on your four years there with pride and gratitude. But *I'm* not *you*. And Wickham is not for me. I have a mission to pursue, and it's going to take all my energy and time to accomplish it. I simply can't afford four years' time devoted to college."

I couldn't help drifting further into my signature sarcasm. "And, may I ask, what great mission will the master, the protégé of the famous U Bo Thet, be embarking on? The great mission that's more important than a college degree?"

Eric smiled broadly. Now that he was a little older, he actually got a kick out of my wry wit. "The protégé of the famous U Bo Thet hasn't figured that out yet. But give him a little time, and he will," Eric said with an exaggerated bow and a flourish of his arm.

I couldn't really blame him. He had absorbed more knowledge from U Bo Thet than any college experience would give him. So, after I could forego my sarcasm and talk honestly again, I gave Eric my blessing to chart his own course into the future. I don't think Eric would have behaved any differently with or without my permission, but he seemed genuinely glad to have it.

He spent his last three years of high school in the vocational track: woodworking, metalworking, and drafting. Eric excelled and dreamed of creating bigger and grander things than the school would allow. He drew scale diagrams of cathedrals, towering sculptures, and elaborate fountains. But reality reigned him in – at least for the time being. He focused on small wood crafts in Dad's old basement workshop. At sixteen, he had gained enough confidence to begin making meticulously crafted mahogany jewelry boxes with brass fittings that sold on consignment at Victoria's Gift Shop on Taylor Street. The boxes sold for $250, and Eric got half. He couldn't make them fast enough and Victoria's waiting list grew, as did her asking price.

But Eric's interest soon turned from jewelry boxes to our house. As we sat together at dinner in the evenings, Eric would unroll blueprints and elevation drawings showing his plans for expanded gardens, a new wing, and cathedral-sized windows. He wanted my permission to begin major renovations on the house and the grounds. I was reluctant, but told him to go ahead. After all, who was I to say no to the brilliant protégé of the famous U Bo Thet?

Chapter 10
Dr. Sanders

In separateness lies the world's great misery,
in compassion lies the world's true strength.
By Gautama Buddha

I should have known. It was inevitable that Eric's unlicensed acupuncture practice would lead to trouble. On a Wednesday evening in August 1995, Dr. Ian Sanders, the father of Eric's friend, Liam, came for a visit. Before I saw him, I could tell by the three insistent rings of our doorbell that someone was upset.

I answered the door while Eric stayed in the kitchen finishing his dinner. Dr. Sanders remained on the porch while I spoke with him. He had just discovered that Eric had been giving acupuncture treatments to one of his patients. This particular patient suffered from severe osteoarthritis and has been scheduled for hip replacement surgery.

"But," said Sanders as he glared at me. "Eric Hill told him he didn't need surgery. Eric Hill told my patient that all he needed was some *Chinese Hocus Pocus* and he would be fine." Dr. Sanders paused a moment to catch his breath. A large vein on his forehead was pulsing visibly. "So, my patient calls this morning to cancel the surgery! He says he feels better and doesn't need it."

"When's the last time you examined this patient?" I asked.

"Three weeks ago, when I explained to him that hip replacement was his only option." Dr. Sanders still glared at me.

"Well, wouldn't it be prudent to examine him again to see if he really is better?"

Dr. Sanders exploded. "Look, that's not the point! Your brother is practicing medicine without a license. He's giving false hope to my patients and discouraging them from getting real medical care. You're his guardian. You have to put a stop to this."

I could see that Dr. Sanders was a little too agitated to reconsider his indictment of Eric. So, I promised him I would speak with Eric. I also asked him again to at least reexamine the patient to see if there was any truth to the claims being made. Sanders grumbled something inaudible and stomped off into the night.

From the kitchen, Eric had overheard everything. I rejoined him at the dinner table. "Eric, you're going to get us both in trouble."

"Don't worry, Sam. When Dr. Sanders sees how limber Clyde Armstrong is now, he'll thank me."

So *that* was Dr. Sander's mystery patient. Sanders had not mentioned his patient's name, but now it all made sense. Clyde Armstrong was a parishioner from our church. he was sixty-eight, had severe arthritis, and used a walker to slowly make his way from his car to the church pew. I had heard that he was planning surgery – Father John had announced it from the pulpit, reminding us all to keep Clyde in our thoughts and prayers. But I had not known he was Dr. Sander's patient. And I certainly didn't know he had since become a patient of Eric Hill, acupuncturist. Eric Hill, the fifteen-year-old unlicensed, untrained acupuncturist, who should be at home doing his schoolwork instead of running around Santa Clara practicing medicine.

I adopted my stern parental voice, the one I use when it's really important that Eric listen. "Eric, even if Clyde *is* better, it doesn't mean we're out of the woods. Practicing without a license is a crime."

"But I don't claim that I'm licensed, Sam. And I don't charge anyone."

"Look, do me a favor and just stop for the time being – at least until this controversy with Dr. Sanders blows over. Then we'll see." Eric nodded with downcast eyes while he continued eating.

Friday afternoon when I came home from work, Dr. Sanders was sitting on our front porch, apparently waiting for me. He stood up when he saw my bicycle approach. "I didn't know you biked to work, Sam. You must save a bundle on gas." His cheery disposition made me immediately suspicious. I responded with a straight face.

"So, what's up now, Dr. Sanders?"

"Can we go inside? I'd rather discuss this in private."

I escorted Dr. Sanders into the house and invited him to have a seat on the sofa. I sat in the facing armchair and waited for him to talk.

"Sam, the most incredible thing has happened. I ran new blood tests and took new x-rays and an MRI on Clyde Armstrong yesterday. I got the results back today. His osteoarthritis is hardly detectable. Previous erosion of his humerus has largely reversed. Damage to the surrounding ligaments, which was clear on an MRI two months ago, is undetectable in the new MRI. Thirty years in medicine and I have never seen anything like this."

"So, does that mean Eric is forgiven?" I asked wryly.

"He's forgiven, but I want to know how he did it. And Sam, between you and me, I have another motive for coming."

Dr. Sanders loosened his necktie and tugged his shirt collar open. He was perspiring although it was comfortably cool in the house.

"Sam, I don't know how to say this delicately so I'm just going to be blunt. I'm dying. I was diagnosed two months ago with pancreatic cancer. Sam, it's just about the worst cancer there is. Extremely virulent, virtually always lethal. I'm taking some drugs that delay the spread, but all I'm doing is buying a few months more."

"Who else knows about this?" I asked, stunned by Dr. Sanders' news.

"Just my wife and Dr. Sedgwick, my oncologist, and several of the staff at Baptist Hospital. We haven't even told Liam yet. But we will have to tell him soon."

A rather long period of silence passed between us. I wasn't sure whose turn it was to talk, and if it was my turn, I had no idea what to say. Finally, Dr. Sanders continued. "I want Eric to treat me, Sam. Look, I know I gave you both a hard time the other day, but that was before I reexamined Clyde. That brother of yours knows something, Sam. I know he can't cure me, but maybe he could reduce the pain or slow the spread of the disease. I know I'm probably chasing a fantasy here, Sam, but I'd just like to try."

Another uncomfortable silence ensued as I considered what I should say. I knew Eric was a talented kid, but this was far more serious than even Clyde's arthritis. I didn't want to give out false hope. Fortunately, I didn't have to respond; just as I opened my mouth to speak, the front door opened and Eric walked in. He eyed Dr. Sanders with curiosity, strode deliberately across the room, and sat in the one remaining armchair.

"What's this about? I stopped doing acupuncture just like you told me, Sam."

"Where did you learn your acupuncture, son?" asked Dr. Sanders, adopting a paternal tone that was a stark contrast from his last encounter with Eric and me.

"It's a long story. And it's a story that I don't talk about much." Eric relaxed back in his chair, sensing, I think, that this visit was about him, but not about fixing more blame.

I chimed in. "Dr. Sanders, Eric and I have an active interest in alternative medical remedies; it's a hobby we both pursue." I certainly did not feel comfortable telling Dr. Sanders the truth. He would think we were both out of our minds.

I'm not sure why that prospect frightened me, but it did.

Suddenly, Eric sat up straight and looked directly at Dr. Sanders. "You're not here to complain about me – you're here because you want my help!" Sanders was startled and didn't answer. Eric glanced quickly at me, looking in my eyes for validation that he was right.

I decided to jump in. "Look Eric, Dr. Sanders was just explaining something to me..."

Eric didn't let me finish. "OK, I see!" It's all coming into focus." He scrutinized Dr. Sander's face as though he were seeing him for the first time. "Now, *you* need *me*." Eric closed his eyes and relaxed into the chair again.

"Does Liam know you're dying?" Eric asked.

Dr. Sanders was visibly flustered. "What makes you think I'm dying?"

Eric's tone shifted. His voice conveyed compassion now. "I could see it in your face – in your eyes. I would guess that Liam has seen it, too. You can't conceal something like this. You should talk to your son."

Dr. Sanders shifted to the front edge of his seat, a cue that he was now ready to level with Eric. "I saw what you did for Clyde Armstrong. It's a miracle. Do you have anything in your bag of medical tricks that can help me?"

Eric rose slowly from his chair and walked across the room. He turned and headed back, only to turn again when he reached us. I had never seen Eric pace a room before. Perhaps, it was a nervous habit reserved for inferior beings like me and the rest of humanity.

Whoops, there goes my sarcasm again.

He stopped on his third trip across the room and spun around to face us both. "I might, but it will cost you."

I was shocked and embarrassed by Eric's retort, and I immediately apologized to Dr. Sanders. Then I glared at my brother. "Look Eric, either help Dr. Sanders or don't, but we're not going to exploit him."

Eric seemed unperturbed as he walked over to Dr. Sanders and stood at the side of his chair looking down at Dr. Sanders' upturned face. "OK, but let me just ask – as a general principle – what would it be worth to you to have your health back?"

Dr. Sanders pushed his chair back so he could look at

Eric without craning his neck. "Life is priceless. You can't put a price tag on it."

"Well, I can. I have a project that I want to pursue. Not for my benefit, but for the community. Only I haven't figured out how to do it yet. It's costly and legally complicated."

Now Eric had piqued my curiosity.

I responded. "Eric, I still object to exploiting Dr. Sanders. But why don't you just tell both of us what you're talking about."

Eric said, "You may have noticed that the house across the street is on the market. The 'for sale' sign went up yesterday. I want to buy that house. I want to buy it and turn it into a hospice, a place where anyone in Santa Clara could come and spend their final days. A place that wouldn't charge a dime; that would be non-profit. A place that would operate entirely from donations. The problem is, I've done some research, and it will take a lot of money to make this idea a reality. It's not just coming up with $550,000 to buy the house. Outfitting it with accessible rooms and medical facilities, hiring licensed staff, getting the property rezoned and licensed, hiring a medical director; all costly and complicated. I'm seventeen—I can't even sign a contract yet. But I want that hospice. And you could help me get it. You've got everything I lack. You've got money; you've got prestige; you've got influence in the community and in the medical profession. You could do it. And you could be the new medical director."

Dr. Sanders was as stunned as I was. Another big idea that Eric had not bothered to share with me. I looked back and forth from Eric to Dr. Sanders. Who was going to speak next?

Dr. Sanders finally broke the silence. "Sure...as long as

we're talking hypothetically, the answer is yes, I would do that. If the choice were to run your hospice for the rest of my life, or to not have a life at all; then I would run your hospice."

"Not hypothetical," Eric said. "My proposal is not hypothetical. This is reality. This is right now. Will you commit to what I have asked? Because if you do, there's no going back."

Dr. Sanders stammered, "I can't believe we're having this conversation."

"That's your choice." Eric turned his back and began heading for the stairs."

"You can't leave!" Dr. Sanders' voice cracked with emotion. I got out of my chair. This whole thing was going too far, and I was going to put a stop to it.

But before I could speak, Dr. Sanders blurted out, "All right! Have it your way. No stipulations. Now, do whatever it is that you do."

Eric turned around, eyed Dr. Sanders curiously and slowly walked back to stand behind the doctor's chair. Dr. Sanders looked nervous.

"Close your eyes and relax." Eric said.

Dr. Sanders shut his eyes, but I don't think he relaxed much.

Eric rubbed the palms of his hands together briskly for a few seconds. He then placed his open palms on either side of Sanders' head, not touching, but hovering an inch or two from his head. He slowly moved his hands down toward Sanders' neck and across his shoulders.

"Lean forward," Eric whispered. Eric moved his palms slowly across Sanders' back.

"Lean back again." Eric moved to Sanders' right side

and used one palm to scan across his face and, the other, his chest. When his right palm reached Sanders' lower waist, it stopped. He held his hand stationary, turning his wrist slightly back and forth. "There's a disturbance right here. Your liver. No, that's not it. It's your pancreas."

Dr. Sanders opened his eyes, obviously surprised. "Keep your eyes closed." Eric moved around to the front of the chair, his legs spread wide, his knees bent to place him at eye level with Sanders. He began moving his hands in a slow broad circle, much like a Tai Chi exercise. Then quickly, he thrust the open palm of his right hand against Sanders' forehand, making a forceful first contact with Sander's body. Sanders kept his eyes closed and Eric continued pressing his palm against Sanders' forehead, while rapidly whispering a chant. I found out later it was a Hindu chant used to exorcise demons. Ten seconds into the chant, Dr. Sanders began shaking...first his head shook from side to side, and then his whole body. Twenty seconds later, he slumped in the chair, motionless.

As Eric finally stepped away, I moved closer. Sanders had passed out.

"Let him rest," Eric said. "He's been through a lot today."

An hour later, Sanders awoke. Eric had retreated to his basement workshop, apparently not particularly concerned about his unconscious patient. He said he needed to finish a jewelry box he had promised to deliver to Victoria's the next day. I shouted down the stairs to let him know Sanders was awake.

"Tell him he can go home," Eric yelled back.

I helped Dr. Sanders collect himself and walked him to the door. I tried to downplay the events of the last two hours. "Dr. Sanders, don't put too much hope in Eric. He's seventeen. He's been experimenting with acupuncture and Chinese herbs and such. He's still learning and he's got some strange ideas. Don't expect too much."

Dr. Sanders looked at me a second, lowered his eyes and nodded. "Yea, I know. Maybe I'm grasping at straws. But you would too if you were me." He walked with a slight limp to his car and drove away.

I went downstairs and joined Eric in his workshop. I couldn't believe how he was able to dissociate himself with the major drama that had just occurred upstairs. He was busy on his jewelry box; at two feet wide; it was the largest one yet. He barely looked up when I entered the room. I sat on the stool in the corner and watched him work for a minute. It was clear that if a conversation was going to happen, it wasn't going to be started by Eric.

So, I began. "How long has this hospice idea of yours been percolating?"

Eric was carefully applying a final coat of lacquer to his masterpiece. "You know, it was U Bo Thet's biggest disappointment. He ministered to many dying people, both as their physician and their meditation teacher. He saw a need for a refuge – a place where they could pursue a careful, conscious death. For fifteen years, he tried to establish a hospice in Rangoon. But he couldn't raise the necessary funds and he couldn't enlist the benefactors that he needed. It seemed odd to me that such a brilliant and accomplished man would fail at such a straightforward goal. When I was tripping and I was inside his skin, I could feel his disappointment. When I returned, I vowed that I would accomplish what U Bo Thet could not. It's another time, and another continent, but I am going to make U Bo Thet's hospice a reality."

"When I was working in the garden last month, Gene Murphy came over to chat. He said he was selling his house and moving to Tampa to be near his sister. He wanted to know if I knew of any potential buyers. I told him I would check and get back to him. I figured out that it was going to take about a million dollars to purchase Gene's house and turn it into a hospice, and I could see that I would run into all the same obstacles that U Bo Thet encountered. So, I've been ruminating over this for a month. Then when Dr. Sanders showed up, looking for my help, I saw it as a sign. I think it's Dr. Sanders' destiny to help me establish the hospice. It's all a sequence of karmic events that are unfolding."

Eric stepped back from his jewelry box, admiring the finished work. He put his brushes in a jar of turpentine to soak overnight.

"At least that's the way I see it. It may look like I was rough with Dr. Sanders, but I was just pushing him to fulfill a destiny that has been in the works for a while. It's why Dr. Sanders was born – it's why he got ill when he did. It's all coming to final fruition."

"But why Murphy's house?" I asked. "Why not a commercial property that's designed and equipped for medical care?"

"With some remodeling, the Murphy house could accommodate twelve residents and two full time staff. That's just the scale I want – not too big, and not too small. Also, since it's right across the street, I can oversee it. I need to make sure it's operated consistently with U Bo Thet's original plan."

"And what about Sanders? Have you cured him?"

"I don't know. I did what I could. I'm counting on a full remission. That's the only way the rest of the plan will succeed. We'll know in a few weeks if his *kundalini* is sufficient."

"Kundalini? What are you talking about?"

Eric removed the heavy cotton apron he was wearing and hung it on the wall hook.

"In the last few weeks, I've been making contact with a different being – someone from a different time and place than U Bo Thet. His name is Ananda. So far, I've been able to piece together that Ananda was born in India around 1845 and that he was a Jain monk of the Dugambara (Sky-clad) sect. He became an itinerant Hindu teacher in his twenties, and during the 1870's he gained a reputation as a Yogic healer. He preached the Hindu belief that everyone has spiritual energy within them called Kundalini. This Kundalini can heal any sickness, but it usually lies dormant at the base of the spine and is never sufficiently activated. If the conditions were right, though, a spiritual master like Ananda could activate it – he did it through a spontaneous act called *Shaktipat*, literally 'touch of universal energy.' Ananda initiated hundreds of followers with Shaktipat. They had to request it, and surrender themselves physically and emotionally to the event. Ananda would strike their forehead with his palm and create a kind of instant enlightenment. When the initiate recovered, he or she would be forever changed. Those lucky enough to receive Shaktipat would remember the event for the rest of their lives – a singular act of grace conferred through their Guru."

Over the following months, Dr. Ian Sanders did indeed achieve a full remission. He was understandably very skeptical and insisted that tests be repeated over and over. It was almost as if he didn't want it to be true. It wasn't until six months later that he finally accepted his cancer was gone. He never did discuss his illness with his son, and he never told anyone –not even his wife or doctors – about his visit to Eric that day. Everyone except Eric and me attributed his recovery to spontaneous remission. Very rare, but not un-heard of. I'm not even sure how Sanders himself viewed his recovery. Did he accept that Eric had healed him? Or did he view it as coincidence?

But what matters is that Dr. Sanders did make good on his promise. He spent a million dollars – half of his net worth – on the house across the street, establishing a non-profit trust, purchasing the house for the trust, and equipping it with all the support systems for a dying clientele. He didn't give up his private practice, but for the next twenty years, he worked half-time as the volunteer medical director of Kin-dred Spirits Hospice. He finally stepped down in 2018. He's seventy-eight years old now, and his health is starting to de-cline again. But he still stops by the hospice every Sunday to see how things are going. If I see him, I step out on the porch and wave.

I spoke with Sanders a lot over twenty years – we talked about the hospice, the patients, and their dying; we talked about everything except the day that Eric performed Shakti-pat on him. I mentioned it once or twice – I wanted to know what he believed. But Sanders would wave me off.

"It doesn't matter what I believe. All that matters is I'm still here, and the hospice needs me." My guess is that Dr. Sanders didn't know what to believe about his recovery. Maybe he changed his life and built Kindred Spirits be-cause it just seemed like the right thing to do.

Postscript: I need to reveal a little more of my own biases. Dr. Andrews cycled this chapter back to me with a hand-written comment. She wrote:

Sam, you've told me a lot about Eric, but not much about you. How did you make sense of what happened? What meaning did you take from it? You know Sam, Virginia Woolf once said, "If you do not tell the truth about yourself, you cannot tell it about other people." Eric Hill's life is indeed fascinating, but to tell it well you need to reveal more of your own truth.

I saw in rereading this chapter that she was right. Something very rare happened in my living room that evening in August, 1995, but I never revealed what it meant to me.

So, let me complete the record now. I had my doubts. I had graduated from Wickham with a degree in religion three months earlier. When I was a junior, I had written a term paper on faith healing. In my research, I found dozens of documented cases of spontaneous cancer remissions following significant religious events – Baptism, visions, laying on of hands by a minister, vivid dreams. The patients inevitably drew a cause and effect relationship in their minds; they were healed because of the spiritual event. But some researchers proposed alternative explanations. One theory is predicated on the fact that a certain tiny percentage of cancers go into remission just as a matter of pure chance. When a victim is fortunate enough to enjoy such a chance remission, there is a natural human impulse to attribute it to divine intervention. Since many people have religious experiences from time to time, it is easy for the healed victim to recall one and say 'That's what caused my remission.'

Another theory is that people who have a great faith in a healer actually heal themselves. Their faith boosts their immune system, their brain generates higher levels of serotonin and endorphins, and their altered body chemistry accomplishes the healing.

Both theories seek a physical explanation other than direct cause and effect between healer and healed. Explanations that rely directly on spirituality or metaphysics never gain credence in scientific circles.

So, my quandary in understanding Dr. Sanders' recovery was finding the likely explanation. Did Dr. Sanders turn out to have a lucky chance remission? Or did Dr. Sander's faith in Eric spur a beneficial healing response? Or did Eric really do what he seemed to do – alter the world in a transcendent way?

I wanted to believe in metaphysics. I wanted to believe that my brother, Eric, was my window into the great beyond. But, if I'm completely honest, I have to say I wasn't sure. And part of my doubts at that time came from lack of data. There were two data points: Clyde Armstrong and Dr. Ian Sanders. If Eric had such miraculous powers, why didn't he go to the cancer ward at St. Luke's Hospital and cure everyone? Why hadn't he stopped the death of Mom and Dad?

In February of 1996, I did ask Eric why he didn't heal more sick people. We were at the breakfast table, and I was reading an article about the growing number of deaths from diabetes and cardio-vascular disease in the American population. I read Eric part of the story and asked him if he thought he could help the victims.

He swallowed a mouthful of corn flakes and said, "Sam, it's a tricky thing. There's an interplay between healer and healed. It's a cooperative dance, and it doesn't always work. If the healer doesn't cooperate, it fails. If the patient doesn't cooperate, it fails. I don't mean cooperate in the sense of doing what you're told. I mean cooperate in the sense of surrendering yourself to the universe."

Eric's explanations were always just like that. Conundrums. They didn't illuminate the cause and effect. His answers just stirred questions around and served them back to whoever was asking.

Chapter 11
Sky Clad

A bodily state, void of all garments of hemp and hair, of
grass, bark, and leaves
and clear of every ornament and covering of decency, a
naked state with the heart
free from every knot of anger and deceit is said to be
sacred nudity.
From *The Jain References in the Buddhist Literature,*
by Acharya Battakera

Eric graduated from high school on June 15, 1996. It was a memorable summer. Bill Clinton was running for re-election as president, Dolly the Sheep was the first mammal to be successfully cloned and a new company, Google, was introduced. But regardless of the momentous events of the time, the most important event for me was the commencement ceremony at Sedalia High School, watching my brother in his blue cap and gown, graduating with the other 247 members of the senior class.

Aunt Ruth drove out to attend; she and I prepared a big dinner that evening for Eric and seven of his friends. I wish Mom and Dad could have been there – they would have been proud of him.

But the celebration was short lived. Beginning the very next day, Eric spent each day in his woodshop in the basement, the sound of power tools reverberating softly through the floors above. He had already established a brisk business in hand-crafted jewelry boxes, chests, and cabinets. With school behind him, he threw himself into it. At least he did for three weeks.

On Friday afternoon, three weeks after Eric's graduation, I came home from work and found Eric standing nude in the middle of the living room, with marks of ash from the fireplace on his face and body. He seemed immersed in thought.

I joked, "Did you forget something – like your pants?"

Eric ignored my joke. He told me he had gone tripping earlier in the day and had found himself looking out through a new pair of eyes. This time the year was 1857, and the eyes belonged to Ananda, the Jain monk in India. Since returning to this life, Eric had spent the day reading about Jainism in the family's old Encyclopedia Britannica. The encyclopedia contained a short article accompanied by a photograph of a Jain monk, his body marked by ash. Eric had used his own ash to duplicate the marks in the photograph.

I knew from my class in comparative religions that Jainism arose in India at the same time as Buddhism, and that the two religions shared many beliefs. In fact, I still had one of college texts on my bedroom bookshelf, M.S. Stevenson's 1915 classic, *The Heart of Jainism*.

Jains embraced an austere life, going so far as renouncing even the simple robes and alms bowl that a Buddhist monk is allowed. Jains would wander about in a state of 'sacred nudity' collecting alms in their cupped hands. The townspeople in rural India, who would be shocked by nudity in an ordinary layperson, viewed the Jains with admiration. Their nudity was not considered an affront; it was esteemed as a sacred calling.

Eric said, "I experienced all that Ananda did for an entire day. He collected alms, gave blessings, delivered a sermon, and performed a healing ceremony. I was especially captivated by the sacred state called 'sky clad.' It was a way of visibly living his renunciation, moment by moment. I returned from the trip two hours ago, and I could still feel that sense of transcendent freedom."

He went on to describe how he stripped and painted his body, thinking it would help to preserve the sublime feelings a little longer. "Unfortunately," Eric admitted, "the feeling is now gone. It's hard to sustain it in the here and now."

I laughed and told him to get dressed. "Maybe this worked in India in 1857, but I don't think the people of Santa Clara are ready for naked monks, and someone could come to the front door anytime." Eric, ignoring my words, closed his eyes and began a slow rhythmic Hindu chant.

"Look," I said, "you need to get dressed and help me – you can't go around the house naked." Eric assented and began dressing.

"Sam, there must be a place where it's ok to be naked."

"Sure, Eric. I've never been to one; they're called nudist camps. But I don't think they are spiritually oriented – it's more about volleyball, swimming pools, and recreation."

"This is important, Sam. Let's see what you can find."

The next day, Saturday, Eric and I rode our bikes to the public library, and searched through the newspaper indexes. We were looking for combined keywords like nudism and religion, or naked and spiritual. The elderly librarian, Mrs. Booch, stopped at our table and asked if she could help us. Eric said, "Why yes, please, we're looking for..."

I waved my hand frantically at him and hissed, turning red-faced with embarrassment. The last thing I wanted was to start a scandal in the public library. I could see Mrs. Booch having fun telling all her friends at church about the strange predilections of the Hill brothers.

"That's ok, Mrs. Booch. I think we have everything we need."

Eric shrugged and buried his nose back in his book.

Five minutes later, I found something in a large, well-worn paperback book called The Holistic Health Directory. The place was Shanti Springs, in the mountains north of the Napa Valley, five miles from Calistoga, California. It was listed as a holistic retreat – featuring yoga, massage, hot mineral springs, and a variety of spiritual workshops; ironically, one of their workshops was on past life regression. Best of all, the description said that the entire property was clothing optional. I showed the page to Eric and he read it with rapt interest before declaring, "This is the place! When can we leave?"

I made a copy of the page, and when we got home, I called and reserved a room for the next weekend. On my calendar, I had reserved that weekend for painting the storage shed in our backyard, but that could wait. I wanted to go with Eric and see what Shanti Springs was all about.

On Saturday morning, when I came down to the kitchen for breakfast, Eric was drinking his coffee and scanning the newspaper. His duffel bag was already packed and stood leaning up against the back door. He looked up and said, "Let's get going."

I grumbled an answer, made a mug of instant coffee, and headed upstairs to pack my own duffel bag. An hour later, after highlighting our route on my AAA Map of California, we were off in our 1986 midnight blue, slightly dented, Chevy van. It was a hundred-mile trip, and after asking for last-mile directions at the Shell Gas Station in Calistoga, we pulled up to Shanti's gate at 11:30 am. The morning weather in Calistoga in August was almost too perfect. The air was cool and clear, wide sky azure with bold stripes of high cirrus clouds. I could immediately sense an unusual energy, even before we passed the gate. There was a vividness, a freshness, to everything I encountered. Partly, this stemmed from the loving decorations that adorned each building, changing it from a building to a living entity. The outside wall of the café featured a life-size mural of a folk singer strumming an acoustic guitar before a scattered audience of eight young girls and boys. The children sat on the floor in a disorganized heap, the younger ones enjoying refuge in the arms and laps of the older. They all joined in the songs. I wondered if the mural depicted what might actually happen inside on any given evening. A nearby cabin featured bright yellow window boxes filled with pots of geraniums and zinnias, soaked in sunlight.

As the gatekeeper flipped through his hand written ledger, looking for our reservation, I noticed he was burning incense in a small brass chalice, which sat on a side table. It took a moment to recognize the scent. "Sandalwood." I said it aloud. The gatekeeper smiled as he handed me the key to our cabin. "Sandalwood and cloves. I burn it each morning. It's hard to be unhappy when your senses are serenaded by sandalwood and cloves."

As we entered the grounds, I felt as if I was seeing ordinary things with new eyes. Two women, with darkly tanned skin wrapped in brightly colored sarongs were stooped over the garden, picking tomatoes. One had her brown hair braided into pigtails. The other wore a frayed blue straw hat. They both looked up at us as we drove by, making eye contact, and delivering cheerful smiles in perfect unison.

By the time I pulled up next to our assigned cabin, I felt transported. I've since learned, after many subsequent visits, that Shanti Springs is just like that. It only takes a moment for the unworldly energy of the place to subsume you.

Shanti describes itself, in its brochure, as a new age religious community. I wasn't sure whether 'religious' was a ploy to cast itself as a church and circumvent property and income taxes, or whether Shanti really was a church – with sermons, dogmas, hymns, and all the other accoutrements that clothed 'real' churches. If it was a church, there was little in the brochure or the grounds to signal its beliefs. I saw only small signs posted throughout asking that we keep our conversations to a whisper, so as not to disturb the tranquility for others. Who knows? Maybe that alone is enough dogma to qualify as a church.

As Eric and I completed a guided tour of the property, led by Melissa, a soulful teenager with a single daisy nestled in her hair, I realized we had arrived at a commune. Shanti Springs had 62 full time residents of all ages who lived there, worked there, and raised children there. It was a classic alternative community, a social experiment based on socialist and egalitarian principles. The 'resort' part of the community was simply the way that many residents earned their livings. Twelve cabins were devoted to visitors who would soak in the mineral baths, dine in the vegetarian café, and enjoy healing massages under the juniper trees. Heaven!

Sprawled across its 200 acres were various houses, community centers, storage facilities, and organic gardens. Although the brochure indicated that the Shanti community was clothing optional, I didn't see anyone practicing nakedness. That is, until we approached the thermal springs. There, a dozen or so nude males and females of all shapes, sizes and ages soaked in the natural mineral water that gushed from the earth into large stone-lined pools, filling the air with steam and sulfur. When the heat was too much, they emerged from the water and reclined unashamed on the pool's edge. Everyone seemed to be following the one explicit rule – that is, they all talked in whispers. The subdued discourse made it all the more peaceful and inviting. But I felt a tug of resistance anyway. I suggested to Eric that we go back to our cabin and unpack.

Eric tossed his duffel bag onto one of the cots, undressed, and set out on a walk by himself. He said he wanted to meditate. He disappeared down a path into the woods, apparently unconcerned that he wore nothing except sandals. What if he got lost? What if he wandered off the property and had to ask for directions back? All the neurotic questions that would have restrained me never seemed to occur to Eric. He was here for twenty-five minutes, and acted like he owned the place.

I wrapped a towel around myself and headed to the hot pool. Feeling bashful, I tried to step into the pool while simultaneously pulling off my towel. It didn't work. I slipped and splashed, attracting everyone's concerned look. I flushed. I would have attracted a lot less attention if I had left my towel in the room. Eric was traipsing all over the property naked, and was probably not registering a glance from anyone. I, trying not to be conspicuous, will probably be the object of giggling among the residents for the next week.

I leaned against the side of the pool and took in the beauty of the place. Thick woods came within a few feet of the pool. Squirrels scampered carelessly right up to the edge – they apparently had not learned to fear the humans here. I saw a fawn through the trees, nibbling on a plant. I felt my muscles relax and felt happy to be here. I didn't know whether Eric was going to find what he wanted here, but I was content.

The next morning Eric and I had massages. Shanti Springs operates its own resident massage school, and it has an excellent reputation. Eric and I lay on tables next to each other in a small outdoor clearing, under the shade of a broad poplar. We relaxed under the ministrations of two young women who were residents of Shanti. Eric, as usual, was naked; I was wearing shorts. I was still feeling hesitant about this whole clothing-optional thing. But the massage was splendid. Melissa, my massage therapist, seemed to know exactly where my tight muscles were. I nearly fell asleep.

After the massage, I went back to the room for a nap; Eric stayed and chatted with the therapists. I woke up about an hour later when Eric returned to the room. "Guess what?" he asked with a broad smile. "I just enrolled in massage school!"

"What? When? How?" I stammered. He explained that he had felt so rejuvenated by his massage that he resolved he would spend the next three months training to be a massage therapist. I knew there was no point in trying to change his mind, so I focused on practicalities. "Don't you need to come home and pack first?" I asked. "I don't need my clothes," he said. "I can attend classes nude. In fact, I don't plan on getting dressed again for the next three months!"

After I packed the car, I wrote a check for six thousand dollars to the Shanti Springs Massage School and said goodbye to Eric. As I drove home, it occurred to me that the purpose of this weekend's trip had completely changed. Eric had started the trip as a way to connect with some ancient Jain named Ananda; it had turned into long-term vocational training in massage therapy. I was angry – I felt like Eric had abandoned me on a whim. But as I got closer to home and had more time to reflect, I realized that underneath the anger was jealousy. I was jealous of the spontaneity that Eric allowed into his life. I could never just change the direction of my life on a whim. Well that's not completely true. The fact is, I wouldn't allow myself to.

Chapter 12
Woodworker, Bodyworker

A disciplined mind brings happiness.
From *the Dhammapada* by Gautama Buddha

Eric graduated from massage school in late August 1996, and settled into a new routine at home. He would read from five to seven in the morning, and then come upstairs and meet me in the kitchen for breakfast. We had an hour every morning to talk before I went to work and Eric headed down to his woodshop. He worked from eight to twelve on his cabinets and handmade furniture. His cabinets were custom-made for affluent customers in San Francisco. The quality was superb, and his reputation spread quickly among the economic elite. By November he had a six-month waiting list.

Each afternoon, from two until four, he would treat a client in his basement therapy room. He had a padded oak table, lots of green plants, soft music, and muted light flowing from the afternoon sun through a stained glass window. Eric's signature two-hour treatment was a mixture of conversation, trigger point therapy, shiatsu, and reiki healing. He would talk quietly with the client as he worked. He avoided long-term clients, telling everyone that he would only give ten treatment sessions. He said that if the problem persisted after ten treatments, they should seek another kind of therapy.

Within ten treatments, Eric had remarkable success. He treated clients with severe cases of fibromyalgia, arthritis, sciatica, and tissue injuries. He also had clients who were suffering from various degrees of depression, bipolar disorder, and anxiety. Five weeks and ten sessions later, their conditions – if not eliminated – were dramatically improved. I was so startled by some of the transformations that I asked him to take before and after photographs to document his work. I spoke with a few of his clients who told me that they could feel energy streaming from Eric's hands. I remember one who had just completed her second session with Eric. She was crying tears of joy – and relief. She had been suffering severe chronic pain and Eric had succeeded where years of surgery and drugs had failed.

I wanted to find out for myself what his clients were experiencing, and asked Eric to work on me. For ten successive Saturday mornings, I experienced firsthand the energy that streamed from his hands. I was amazed as waves of heat coursed through my body wherever he touched. My only basis of comparison was the massage I had received at Shanti Springs six months earlier. However, Eric's treatment was totally unique. A chronic pain that I had in my right knee from a high school soccer injury disappeared after two treatments and has never returned. Unfortunately, he held me to the same rule for all his clients – ten visits maximum.

Eric earned quite a bit of money between his woodwork and bodywork. He tossed everything he earned into a bedroom drawer. When I was getting dressed for an alumni dinner at Wickham, I looked into Eric's dresser, searching for a pair of cufflinks – I hate formal attire. I didn't find cufflinks but I found over $30,000 in cash and checks. Some of the checks were six months old and had never been cashed. I scooped up the contents of the drawer and, clutching the money in my fist, descended two flights of stairs to the basement. Eric was in his workshop, busily applying a second coat of varnish to a mahogany armoire. I waved the money at him. "Eric, you can't leave this loose in your dresser drawer! It has to go in the bank." Without looking up he said, "I don't want to deal with it. You take it." I sighed, shook my head, and started back up the stairs.

As I got back to my bedroom, I wondered to myself, *why do I let Eric foist things on me like that? Why don't I push back?* But I quickly reoriented myself. *After all,* I thought, *it's not like he's lazy. He works very hard at his furniture business and his bodywork business. And he makes a lot of money. If he wants me to take care of the finances, then I will.*

Ever since that afternoon confrontation in Eric's workshop, I check Eric's drawer once a week, remove any money I find and put it in the bank. With his earnings, I pay all of Eric's bills – his share of the utilities, phone, repairs, and groceries. I even enrolled Eric in an HMO health plan and I pay his monthly premiums.

When I did Eric's tax return, I was surprised at his income. In 1996, he earned $80,000 from his combination of woodwork and bodywork. It was sobering to realize that my little brother, without a college education, made more money working six hours a day from home than I did working full-time for the Postal Service.

As the months passed during 1997, I became resigned to the fact that, for all the bureaucratic tasks of life, I would be a caretaker for Eric. He wanted to be free to focus on what he loved – woodworking, bodywork, and tripping. What hadn't become clear to me yet was that Eric would soon also become my caretaker. I saw the magic that he worked on his clients. And I saw the extraordinary insights he was gaining from his encounters with death. But I didn't yet comprehend who Eric was becoming.

In June, 1997, Eric informed me that he planned to attend a day-long meditation session scheduled to be held in a Buddhist temple in Los Gatos. Even though I had no idea what to expect, I was intrigued and decided to join him in the session. Two weeks later, Eric and I climbed into our van for the hour-long drive.

The temple was a small building tucked away in a grove of Eucalyptus. It was staffed by four Sri Lankan monks who worked under the direction of the abbot, a slight old man with sparkling eyes named Chandrika Bodhigoda. He insisted that western visitors call him 'Chandy.' He had joined a monastery in Sri Lanka when he was twenty-five, and had been practicing Theravada Buddhism for forty-five years. Chandy greeted us both warmly, and seemed immediately interested in Eric.

After a quick tour of the temple, the meditation session began. Eric and I were handed cushions and invited to sit on the floor with about twelve others who I learned were all long-time students of Chandy's. I closed my eyes and tried to follow Chandy's instructions. He told us to keep our backs straight and focus our attention on our breath – noticing each in-breath, each out-breath, and the touch of the breath as it makes contact with the nose. Ten minutes of absolute silence ensued. Then Chandy interrupted the silence by repeating exactly the same instructions. "You may notice your mind wandering. If you do, just bring your attention back to the breath. Back to the point where your breath makes contact with the nose."

I found the instructions monotonous and difficult. I couldn't keep my attention on my nose for more than a second. I soon gave up trying. Instead of meditating, I mentally reviewed my household chores for the next week. After that, I tried to remember the names of every teacher I had from kindergarten through college. After that, I tried to remember the Spanish words for kindergarten and college. My mind was skipping from one task to the next. From the outside, I must have looked like I was meditating; from the inside, I was doing everything but.

I glanced over at Eric. He was sitting very still. Knowing him, he had probably locked his attention on his breath twenty minutes ago and had never let it waver. For a moment, I thought he had also stopped breathing; but then I saw a slight rise and fall of his chest and knew he was still among the living. It occurred to me at that moment that I was more interested in finding out about Eric's experience of meditation than I was in doing it myself.

Chandy interrupted the silence of the room once again. "If you find your attention wandering, just notice the lapse. Then bring your attention back to your breath. If you feel pain anywhere in your body, just notice the pain sensation. Then, without judgment, bring your attention back to your breath."

At the end of an hour, Chandy sounded a small chime to signal that the meditation period was over. Eric rose and stretched and walked over to Chandy. He gave a respectful bow and spoke quietly with his new teacher. I grabbed my note pad and began writing down all the chores that I had been mentally listing over the last hour.

Later, on the way home in the car, I asked Eric about his meditation. "It went well," he said. "I saw lights of different colors within a few minutes, and began feeling a sense of euphoria sweeping over me. How was it for you?" I admitted that I had not been able to follow Chandy's instructions at all.

Eric continued. "I followed his instructions, but the way I would describe my experience was different from his instructions. I noticed that my attention to my breath was intermittently interrupted by a thought. I found that a subtle shift occurred in me – I was less interested in the occasional thought and more interested in the space between my thoughts. I noticed that in these quiet spaces, my mind would start to open up and I felt like I was floating in boundless space. When this blissful experience was interrupted by a stray thought, it was a bit of a let-down."

"So how does it compare with going on a trip?" I asked.

"I didn't make contact with other beings during meditation, but otherwise it was similar," Eric replied. "The sense of relaxation, the suspension of mental activity, the feeling of floating. The similarity made me wonder – is it really necessary to die in order to be with other beings like Ananda and U Bo Thet? Maybe I could reach them through deep meditation."

For the next six months Eric went to the Temple every day. He preferred to go at 5 am to meditate with Chandy and the four monks. Chandy was not accustomed to guests at the first sitting of the day, but he received Eric warmly and invited him to stay for tea after. I suppose I could have gone with Eric since my job at the post office didn't start until eight, but I was not enthusiastic about meditation. I knew that if I went, I would spend the whole hour chasing a stream of my own thoughts; I figured I could do that anywhere without help.

As Eric progressed in meditation, he explained to me that what we had learned the first day was called *Anapanna* meditation – used to develop mental concentration. It was only a first step towards the more advanced meditation technique called *Vipassana*. On his second visit, Eric began learning Vipassana from Chandy.

Eric was told, "Maintain your concentration but move your attention from the nose to the top of your head. Now move your attention through your neck, your shoulders, arms, and hands." For one full hour, Eric practiced slowly sweeping his attention throughout his body part by part. The object of concentration is the constant flux of bodily sensations – what Buddhists call *amicca*, a Pali word for which there is no exact English equivalent.

Eric explained this to me.

"Chandy told me the goal is to experience the illusory character of the self. To notice that what we call the self, what we call our body, what we call our mind – they are all just rapidly changing phenomena. Nothing is constant – not even for an instant. There is nothing to hold on to. He said that eventually I would reach a point where boundaries dissolve and I experience my body as just a stream of energy, undifferentiated from the surrounding world. The energy stream flashes in and out of existence millions of times per second. According to Chandy, as one 'tunes in' to this energy stream, one realizes that this concept we have of 'self' is nothing more than turbulent energy, continuously arising, and continuously dying."

"What I'm noticing is that my practice of Vipassana has reduced my desire to go on trips." Eric continued. "Somehow the Vipassana is filling my spiritual needs. I haven't tried using Vipassana to reach U Bo Thet and Ananda, but somehow I think with continued effort, I will be able to."

The next day when I came home from work, I was helping Eric set up chairs for the inner circle that evening. Eric said, "Well I did it – I launched into a trip without dying first."

I was immediately interested. "How? You got there with Vipassana?"

"Yes, Eric answered. "I was deep in Vipassana and instead of keeping my attention within my body, I let it move outside of my body. Within a few minutes, I was actually floating above my physical body looking down on it. I got so excited by what was happening that I would start thinking, and as soon as I thought about what was happening, I snapped back into my body."

Eric continued. "With practice, I was spending a minute or two at a time outside of my body. Near the end of the hour I moved my attention directly into Chandy's body. The experience was identical to the trips I had made to U Bo Thet. I could experience reality from Chandy's viewpoint; I felt his breathing. I could feel him doing his Vipassana, sweeping his attention through his body. I wanted to see if I could see through Chandy's eyes and silently willed his eyes to open. His eyes opened but as soon as they did, I found myself right back in my own body."

"After he rang his chime and dismissed the monks, Chandy pulled me aside and admonished me. He told me that I shouldn't be going outside of the body. He said that while I am under his instruction, I must scrupulously follow his directions."

"So, what are you going to do? I asked.

Eric didn't hesitate. "I'm going to follow Chandy's instructions. He's my teacher; what else can I do?"

Chapter 13
A Career for Sam Hill

Before enlightenment, chop wood and carry water.
After enlightenment, chop wood and carry water.
From *The Sayings of Layman Pang* by Layman Pang

My senior year at Wickham was filled with indecision. What would I do with my degree? What could a person do with a degree in Philosophy and Religion? My father's words haunted me – I could still see him holding up the classified ads from the Sunday paper – "Not many listings for philosophers, Sam." It had been funny when he said it. It was his signature wry wit.

But it wasn't funny now. I had gone to college to pursue my passion, not to train for a job. But with six months left before graduation, I began to doubt myself. Now that I had pursued my passion, what happened next?

I graduated from Wickham College on June 14, 1995. Eric came to watch me walk across the stage in my cap and gown. As a Summa Cum Laude, I was third to graduate. At the honors reception after graduation, one of my professors, Max Stillman, came to shake my hand. I introduced him to Eric. Max said, "Eric, you have to convince this stubborn brother of yours to stay in school. He has the potential to get his PhD. I've told him sever-

al times that I would write him a letter of recommendation – I think I can get him a graduate teaching assistantship as well."

Max was making his pitch to Eric because he had not been able to persuade me. It was actually a very kind offer. When Max learned that my parents had died, he came to the funeral. He also sort of adopted me. He had two grown sons of his own – both of whom had attained their PhDs and were teaching in east coast colleges. I think in his eyes I was his number three son, ready to be molded into yet another academic.

"Max, I've been immersed in books for four straight years – I was thinking of doing something else for a change; get a job, work with other people."

"Sam, teaching is a job. It's a job where you work with lots of other people. You have a brilliant mind – don't waste it on some humdrum job. *Use* your mind."

I searched for words – what could I say to Max? How could I make him understand?

Eric interjected. "Dr. Stillman, what's the better way to understand the mystic's path – to read about it? Or to follow it?"

Max seemed delighted by the invitation to debate. "The best way is to do both. The choices are not mutually exclusive. Most of the professors in the religion department not only study religion, but also practice it. The two activities reinforce each other."

Max now had captured Eric's keen interest. He began looking at Max with intense curiosity, probing his eyes, looking for who was inside.

"You practice Buddhism!" Eric blurted out. "You are a monk!"

Max seemed unperturbed. "Yes, I have been practicing

Buddhist meditation for fifteen years. And yes, two years ago, I went through the formalities of ordination as a monk. How did you know that? Very few people know that about me. In fact, I purposely took ordination after the school year was over so that I wouldn't have to explain my shaved head to my colleagues here. It is still, after all, a Catholic college."

"Who is your teacher?" Eric asked, now quite serious.

"First, you answer my question; then I'll answer yours." The inquisitive attitude that I had seen Max use in the class-room was coming out. "How did you know that I was an or-dained Buddhist monk? I never told Sam."

Eric smiled. He took a step closer to Max, his gaze fixed on Max's face. "OK. I'll tell you. I knew the same way I know that you recently had a heart attack. A mild heart attack, but it really frightened you. You've been thinking a lot about death for the last three months, haven't you?"

Max stepped back, obviously startled. "Say, what kind of game is this?"

I motioned for Eric to hush. He was digging a hole that I did not want to go down. "Max, ignore Eric. My little brother is always pulling stuff like this. It's his way of trying to get attention."

Max had taken off his glasses and was wiping his fore-head with his handkerchief. He appeared much calmer now. "No Sam, you're not going to dismiss me that easily. You've opened up Pandora's Box here. I want to know what's happening."

I took a deep breath. I couldn't lie to Max. I lied to my own Dad about Eric. And he died before I ever got the chance to tell him the truth. I wasn't going to let it happen again.

"Okay Max. Here it goes. Eric has been entering deep

mystical trances for over five years. Like near death experiences. While in trances, he's made past life regressions. He's learned a lot in the process. And one of the skills he's acquired is that, when he puts his mind to it, he can literally read a person like a book. If someone has been preoccupied with death, Eric can sense it almost like reading the person's thoughts."

Max looked at Eric, as if seeking some kind of validation. Eric just nodded.

"Sam, this is incredible. You should have told me before. Don't you see the opportunity we have here? We can study what's happening to Eric and unlock secrets that no one has ever been privy to."

Now it was my turn to smile. "Max, that's exactly what I've been doing for five years. I have sixteen notebooks full of records. And that's what I plan to do instead of going to graduate school. I want to spend my time hanging around with Eric – to see how much I can learn of what he knows."

Max was at a loss for words. Eric rescued him. "Look, Dr. Stillman. You're obviously interested in finding out more about me. And I want to know more about you. I want to know more about your teacher. More about your meditation practice. And your ordination. Why don't you come to our house for dinner on Friday? I'll answer all of your questions then, and you can answer mine."

I had never seen Max so excited. He grabbed the notepad from inside his jacket, fumbled with his pen, and carefully wrote down our address and phone number. He shook both our hands a little too long. He was clearly affected.

In the summer of 1999, Eric made the transition from meditation student to meditation teacher. In accordance with Buddhist custom, he asked Chandy for permission to teach. Such a request is no small matter. In the Theravada tradition, gaining permission from one's own teacher is a guarantee of sorts. It means that you become part of a continuous lineage that reaches all the way back to the Buddha himself.

In actuality, some links within this long lineage become lost or forgotten. When he gave Dharma talks, Chandy often included stories about his teacher and his teacher's teacher. But he could not recall the name of his teacher's teacher's teacher.

"But I know nevertheless that the chain is unbroken," Chandy said. "Everyone who taught in the past had to have permission from their teacher. And permission could only be given by one who had received permission. This is a cardinal rule of Buddhism. No monk would ever disgrace himself by teaching without permission. No one that is, except for a Buddha. A Buddha is self-enlightened, and is born to teach."

Eric knew that a request to teach was a solemn matter. He invited Chandy to dinner at our house. After dinner, while we sat in the living room with tea, Eric spoke. "Master, I wish to teach. I seek your permission."

Chandy smiled and relaxed back into his chair. "What is it you wish to teach, Mr. Hill?"

Eric hesitated slightly. "The path. I want to teach the path that leads to freedom. I want to teach morality, concentration, and wisdom. I want to show people the fruits of meditation."

"You have been in my instruction but a single year. What makes you think you are ready to teach others?"

"Master, I have lived countless lives, developing my paramis, keeping my vows. I have disciplined my mind through meditation for six hundred years. I have completed much preparation."

Chandy sipped his tea, allowing several seconds of silence. "Then you shall teach. You shall teach with my blessing. But you shall not be a lay teacher. I want you to ordain as a monk."

Eric pressed his palms together and bowed. "Master, I would be honored to join the community of monks. I ask that you ordain me."

Chandy reached out and touched Eric's head. "Sunday after next. We will have an ordination ceremony at the temple."

Chandy looked up at me. "And Sam. Will you also take ordination?"

I was flustered. I didn't expect the question. I wasn't supposed to become the object of this conversation. I had planned only to listen.

"Chandy, I have not made the preparations that Eric has."

Chandy laughed. A full belly laugh that went on for several seconds. As he laughed, he looked at Eric, who stifled a smile. I was more flustered.

When he regained his composure, Chandy said, "Sam, you don't have to be a saint to join the Sangha. You just have to be a seeker of truth. I will give you a robe, sandals, and an alms bowl. You will kneel while I shave your head. The shaving of the head symbolizes your renunciation of attachments to worldly things. When this is complete, I will summon you as a monk with the Pali command, 'Ekku Bhikku'. It means 'Come forward, monk.' Then we will have a celebration meal with the other monks. That's all there is to it. You can return to lay life the next day if you wish. But for the rest of your life, for every breath you take, you will also be a Bhikku."

I looked back and forth between Eric and Chandy. "Yes, Master, I wish to ordain."

Chandy clapped his hands together with glee. "Then it's settled, I will see both of you in two weeks. You will enter the temple as householders, you will leave as Bhikkus."

We walked Chandy outside to his car and watched silently as he drove away. After his car had disappeared from sight, Eric said "Sam, life just keeps getting more interesting all the time, doesn't it?"

"I guess I had not thought until tonight about officially declaring myself a Buddhist, Eric. Whenever anyone asked me my religion, I always said Episcopal. I guess once I ordain, I won't be able to say that anymore."

"In all my lives, I think I've been Episcopal, Catholic, Jewish, Sufi, Hindu, and Jain; Eric said. And in this life and the last, I am a Buddhist. For me, there's no conflict. They're all paths to the same truth. It's who you are that's important, not how you label yourself."

I nodded silently. "I'm going in to clean up from dinner, Eric."

Eric was now absorbed in the moon. It was a clear night sky and a radiant moon. "Start washing," Eric said. "I'll be there in a moment to dry."

That night, I brought my college Buddhism texts to bed with me. For an hour, I reviewed the chapters dealing with the Buddhist Sangha. That night, I dreamed of Bhikku Sam wandering the village with his begging bowl, making alms rounds. I could see the gratitude of the villagers as they put rice in my bowl. Feeding a monk is an opportunity to make great merit – something worldly is given, something divine is received. It was a sweet dream.

Chapter 14
The Kidnapping

True knowledge exists in knowing you are nothing.
From *Apology* by *Plato,* Socrates

Eric had stopped tripping, out of deference to his meditation teacher. To celebrate six months under Chandy's instruction, Eric invited him and the four monks to lunch at our house. Eric and I spent the whole morning preparing authentic Burmese dishes. As we worked in the kitchen, Eric talked about life in Burma.

"Lay people can't afford to meditate all day; they have jobs and families that keep them busy. The way that lay people support their religion is by feeding the monks. The monks leave their monastery each morning and carry their alms bowl silently through the streets. Residents of the town are ready for their arrival and come outside with food. It is given in silence to the monk followed by a bow with hands pressed in a prayer position. As a layperson makes the offering to the monk, he feels in that moment that he is a vital participant in the monk's spiritual quest. The monk could not live long without alms, so when he meditates, he shares his blessings with the community that supports him."

When Chandy and his monks arrived, Eric and I treated them all with the reverence they would get in Burma. We brought out bowls of steamed rice, curries, and chutney. We bowed respectfully, and stood by as they tasted the foods and smiled with approval. We didn't join them until Chandy motioned for us to sit down. Chandy was obviously pleased with our cooking and our attention to etiquette. As I ate with Eric and the monks, I thought about the importance of simple ritual. The simple ritual of feeding monks every morning in Burma gives structure and meaning to millions of lives. And as I performed the same simple ritual in my kitchen in Santa Clara, California I felt my body relax and my spirit rise. It's a simple ritual, connecting with the community of monks. Simple and powerful.

I didn't see Chandy again for about a month. On a Saturday in August 1998, Chandy telephoned our house. Eric was working downstairs, and I took the call in the kitchen. Chandy was agitated, and that surprised me. He had always been so serene whenever I encountered him before; I had assumed that he never got upset. Now he suddenly seemed all too human.

Chandy said he wanted to see Eric and me at the temple right away. When I told Eric, he didn't ask any questions. We both set out in the van, and drove for an hour without saying a word. What could we say? Chandy had not told me what was wrong, but it had to be serious.

One of the monks met us in the driveway and showed us into the shrine room. Eric and I sat quietly on the floor at Chandy's feet. Chandy once again looked calm – the distress I heard on the phone was gone; but I could still detect some concern in his eyes.

"A child had been abducted. An eight-year-old boy. The

boy's parents are members of this temple; they have been practicing meditation here for two years. Tom and Clara Donavan have also donated generously to the work of this temple. In fact, their donation paid for the new meditation hall. They awoke yesterday morning to find their son, Adam, missing from his bed. The police have searched in vain for the last 36 hours."

Chandy explained that the FBI was now involved, and that someone claiming to have kidnapped Adam was asking for a $10 million ransom. The Donovans, devastated by their loss, pleaded with the FBI to let them pay, but the Special Agent Christy St. James, who was heading the investigation, strongly discouraged them. She said the profile of the crime fit two other kidnappings in California, one three years earlier and one five years earlier. In both cases the victims had been killed after the ransom was delivered. Agent St. James said that Adam had a better chance of survival if the ransom was withheld.

I was stunned that Chandy's meditation students would have the ability to pay $10 million to anyone. I found out later that the Donovans came from wealthy families and were both prominent citizens in the town of Santa Clara; Tom was president of Citizens Bank and Clara was founding director of the Actors' Theater.

Tom and Clara called Chandy for support early this morning. Chandy went to the Donovan home, accompanied by two of his monks. Chandy tried to comfort the Donovans while the two monks sat in the corner of the living room floor and chanted prayers for Adam. When they returned to the temple mid-day, Chandy phoned Eric.

Finally, Chandy explained why he had summoned Eric and me to the temple; he wanted Eric to find Adam Donovan.

Eric must have made quite an impression on Chandy seven months before when he had traveled out from his body and into Chandy's consciousness. Seven months ago, Chandy had told Eric to cease all such activities. Today, Chandy wanted Eric to leave his body to search for Adam.

Eric said, "Of course I want to help, but what can I do? I don't know how to do what you ask."

Chandy said, "I can guide you. I don't have your ability, but I can be your guide." Eric nodded with resignation and closed his eyes, preparing to die. "No, no!" said Chandy. "You won't find him that way. You need something that belongs to the boy to sharpen your intuition. We must go to the boy's home." Chandy led us outside to my van and directed me as I drove to the Donovan family's home.

When we arrived, we had to get past a cordon of police and FBI before we were introduced to a very distraught Tom Donovan; Clara was sedated in bed. Chandy asked if there was unwashed clothing that had been recently worn by Adam. Tom found a t-shirt in the laundry room – it was a Muppets t-shirt emblazoned with a picture of Kermit the Frog on the front and Miss Piggy on the back. Eric took the shirt, glanced at Chandy, and instinctively seemed to know what to do. He took the t-shirt and pressed it against his face, feeling the texture; smelling the scent. He continued to hold it to his face as he went into meditation. After a minute, he entered a deep trance and his breathing became nearly undetectable.

Nearly thirty minutes passed in complete silence, Eric motionless on the floor. The only way I knew Eric was alive was the very subtle motion of his chest as he breathed. I was becoming more uncomfortable with each passing minute.

What was Eric doing? Nothing seemed to be happening. The FBI agents eyed Eric with some suspicion. They even started to approach, but Tom Donovan motioned them away.

Then Eric opened his eyes. His eyes were wet with tears and he smiled brightly through them. He reached up and grasped Tom Donovan's hand tightly. "Your son is in police custody. I'm not sure where exactly, but the police have him."

I was watching Tom Donovan and could tell that he didn't know how to react, or what to say. I don't think Tom knew whether to believe Eric or not. He had only agreed to this experiment because of his trust in Chandy. As Tom stood with his hand in Eric's hand, tears filled his eyes but I could also sense his doubt.

Five minutes later the Donovan's phone rang. It was the police department in Santa Barbara. They had pulled a car over on a traffic stop and had recognized Adam Donovan as the passenger in the car. With his doubt dispelled, Tom's tears came gushing and he ran upstairs to tell his wife. A minute later he came running back downstairs – he hugged both Eric and Chandy and kept repeating "Thank you."

I was happy for the Donovans but wasn't sure what had happened. Had Eric done something to save the boy, or did he just have a premonition that the police had found Adam? In other words, was he the hero or just the messenger?

In any case, I always think of August 11, 1998 as the beginning of the Inner Circle. Tom and Clara invited Eric and me to dinner at their house that Friday. Eric enchanted them with stories of U Bo Thet and Ananda. But Eric never volunteered information about the day of Adam's rescue and the Donovans didn't ask. I noticed that Adam Donovan seemed to have an intuitive sense that Eric was a special friend –

he spontaneously hugged Eric, pressing his face into Eric's chest. Me? I got a handshake.

Eric returned the courtesy by having the Donovans over to our house for dinner the following Friday. We all talked nonstop for three hours about life, death, Buddhism, and meditation. The Donovans came to our house for dinner every Friday for the next four years.

The Donovans told others at the Buddhist temple about the Friday evening gatherings. Eric was soon getting phone calls from people asking if they could bring a dish and join in the conversation. By September, the circle had grown to ten people.

I did ask Eric, when we were alone at home the evening of Adam's rescue, how he knew that Adam was safe. Eric said:

> 'It took me about fifteen minutes to reach a sufficiently deep sense of concentration. Then I began to see lights. One purple, one orange, and one blue. I wasn't sure which light to follow. I could dimly hear Chandy's voice calling 'Follow your intuition to the boy,' and I could smell Adam from the t-shirt I was holding over my mouth. As strange as it sounds, the purple light seemed to smell like the t-shirt. I went closer and the scent got stronger. Finally, I entered the light, immersing myself in it, and started to emerge on the other side.
>
> Suddenly I was in a pickup truck on the freeway. I was sitting in the passenger seat and a burly man in overalls was sitting next to me driving. I caught a glimpse of myself in the side mirror – I was Adam! Or at least I was inside his consciousness. I could sense Adam's terror. I tried to will him to grab the keys from

the gunman, but his fear was too great. When Adam turned his head to the left, I could see through his eyes the way to his rescue. A police care was two cars over on the freeway.

I carefully maneuvered my attention out of Adam's body, out of the truck, and across the freeway to the police cruiser. I approached the driver, a burly cop with a bushy mustache and eyes hidden by sunglasses. I entered his body and immediately sensed his thoughts. I tried to direct his attention to the pick-up truck; he didn't respond well. I succeeded in causing him to glance at it several times, but he made no other action. I was feeling stymied.

His partner was a woman, pretty, who appeared to be Latina, maybe somewhere in her thirties. I left the male's body and moved toward her. As I entered her, I sensed immediately that she was silently praying. Like before, I tried to direct her attention to the pickup and I also tried to convey a feeling of danger to her. She responded much better than her partner had. I guess it was because she had been praying: she must have thought I was God communicating to her.

She said to her partner, "Stan, pull over that blue pickup. Something's not right." Her partner was reluctant – he wanted to know the reason. At this point, Sonia – the policewoman – became agitated. "Stan, just pull him over! You've got to trust me on this one!" Stan flipped on the light and siren and maneuvered behind the pickup. He said to Sonia, "We'll tell him that one of his brake lights is out. That will give you a chance to talk to him and satisfy your concern."

The truck did not try to escape its pursuer; it

pulled over and the man in the driver's seat leaned out the window with a quizzical look. At this point, Sonia saw a boy through the rear window of the truck and could see his face reflected in the truck's side mirror. She grabbed her log book from the back of the cruiser and pulled out the picture of Adam that the FBI had broadcast that morning. Adam is blonde and the boy in the truck was dark-haired but she dismissed the inconsistency – I guess police are trained to expect kidnappers to disguise their victims. She got out of the car, a gun drawn but pointed down by her side, walked over to the passenger side of the truck and yanked the door open. She squinted a bit since she was now facing into the sun and asked, "Are you Adam Donovan?"

The boy leapt from the truck and into Sonia arms. "Yes!"

"Eric, you're a hero! You saved Adam's life!"

Eric touched my shoulder and said, "I'm nothing more than an informant. The police saved Adam – they confronted the kidnapper; they risked their lives. All I did was tip them off."

"But what about the reward? By all rights, you earned the reward."

Eric only replied, "If anyone deserves the reward, it's Chandy. I wouldn't have known how to locate Adam without his guidance."

Chapter 15
Renovation and Refuge

The jewel of community, the Sangha, is to be held equal to the Buddha and the Dharma. Indeed, the whole of the holy life is fulfilled through spiritual friendship.
by Gautama Buddha

The six Victorian style homes on Blackbird Court had similar interiors with small functional areas – a parlor, a formal dining room, a galley kitchen, and five small bedrooms – suitable for a large family. Over the last fifty-two years, the elms that lined the street have grown to towering heights, cloaking both the street and the six homes from sun and wind. The value of the homes has also grown to towering heights – this house that my parents paid $20,000 for in 1968 is now worth over one million dollars.

Of course, half of that value is due to Eric's extensive renovation. A 30-year old house with creaky floors and weather-beaten siding became a showplace. Eric added a new wing and a sweeping tiered redwood deck. He knocked down interior walls and created grand rooms with twelve-foot ceilings. Soaring skylights lit the house by day and revealed the stars at night. Every room was fitted wall-to-wall with the fine mahogany cabinets that were Eric's specialty. On the property outside, he created magnificently landscaped and terraced gardens, cooled by fountains, and bursting with color from sixteen varieties of roses.

Just as Eric was finishing the renovation on our house, Ron Sharp, who owned the house across the street, decided to sell. Before he listed it with a realtor, he asked Eric and me if we were interested.

Eric told me that he wanted to establish a monastery. He said Chandy intended to expand his outreach by establishing a new monastery and teaching center in Santa Clara. The only thing lacking was a suitable space.

"Chandy told me that if we could locate affordable space for him, he would move to Santa Clara to establish a teaching monastery," Eric explained. "He said he would turn over the Los Gatos Temple to Adnanda, his senior assistant."

Eric elaborated on his idea of establishing a religious foundation on Blackbird Court. Ron Sharp's house would be the first element of the foundation. Chandy and five monks would move in and begin teaching meditation to the people of Santa Clara. Eventually, Eric said, we would acquire the other homes on Blackbird Court and expand the Foundation.

I didn't support the idea. I felt the job of establishing a new church should be a broad-based congregational effort, not the work of one person. But I told Eric that half of our parents' estate belonged to him, and it was enough to buy the house if he wanted.

A week later it was done. David Leary, an attorney friend of Eric's, had accomplished all the paperwork to establish the Triple Refuge Foundation, and purchase the house as a foundation asset. As a registered church, Triple Refuge would pay no income or property taxes – a huge savings. Eric and three friends did some remodeling inside the house to make it suitable for a monastery. By December, Chandy and three monks had moved in and were holding their first classes.

Eric approached Mike Evans, who lived next door, about his next acquisition. Mike was a widower who lived alone, and had talked for years about moving to Phoenix so he could be near his sister. He accepted Eric's offer of $520,000 and Eric, using our home as collateral, borrowed the money. It became the Misty Moon Seminar Center, with Chandy's meditation classes on the main floor, and an alternative health clinic in the basement. The upper floors were remodeled into workshop rooms for vegetarian cooking classes, yoga, and massage classes.

One of the massage therapists who rented a studio in Misty Moon was Tanya Cerhard. She was a 34-year-old former tax accountant, who now split her time between doing massage and raising two foster children. As Eric got to know her, he discovered her ambition to establish a group home for foster children. She felt she could help more children if she only had a suitable space. This led to the third house, Children's Castle, being added to Triple Refuge. In March, 2000, all three buildings were humming with activity. Misty Moon was covering all of its costs through rental revenues and class fees. Children's Castle was getting some support from Santa Clara County office of children's services.

Eric said at the March Board Meeting that he wanted to purchase the remaining two homes on Blackbird Court by March, 2001. He wanted to establish a women's shelter in one. Eric finished the renovation of our house in November, 2000. That same month, he bought the house across the street. In 2000 he bought the house next door, and two years later, using a generous $2 million donation from Thomas Donovan, he bought the other three houses on Blackbird Court. Actually, the houses were purchased by the non-profit Triple Refuge Foundation. But while Eric was alive, he and Triple Refuge were one and the same. He created it; he ran it; and he expanded it. One house became a seminar center, one a hospice, one a shelter for battered women, one a home for foster children, and one a small Buddhist monastery for Chandy and his six monks. Of the six houses on Blackbird Court, only ours was not owned and dedicated to Triple Refuge.

Every Friday, beginning in 1998, Eric and I held dinner gatherings at our house. As the gathering became well-established, we wanted to give it a name. Initially we thought of calling it 'Every Friday.' But this seemed too banal, and we settled on the name 'Circle of Friends.' In conversation, it was just 'The Circle.' Twenty or more people would attend, sitting on cushions in our living room, enjoying a vegetarian meal. But the meal wasn't what drew The Circle together. After the meal, Eric would spend an hour giving an impromptu 'Dharma talk.' We never knew what he would talk about; I don't think Eric knew. But he would meditate for a minute while we watched, open his eyes slowly and look around like he was seeing us all for the first time. Then he would talk. Sometimes he shared an experience he had; sometimes he asked questions. As Eric talked, the stillness in the room was extraordinary. People were pulled onto a different plane. Some laughed, others dabbed tears from their eyes. Everyone was sorry it had to end at ten o'clock. Most would have gladly listened to Eric talk about life, death, and rebirth late into the night.

I'll never forget one particular story that Eric shared at a Circle meeting. His topic was 'Thinking Has to Stop.'

'Here's what I notice about myself. I have become addicted to tripping. Especially when I visit with U Bo Thet, I have the feeling of flow. U Bo Thet's mind is so concentrated and present; it's like a constant high.

Then, when I return to being Eric, it's something of a letdown. I'm back to a state of restlessness and worry, of thinking about appointments I had yesterday or appointments coming up tomorrow. I think about a letter I have to write or letters that I still haven't read.

When I take inventory of my thoughts in a day, they're usually the same thoughts that occurred the previous day, and the same thoughts that will occur the next day. That's not to discount the importance of such thoughts. I have to think about my massage clients and their appointments, and I have to think about my cabinetry customers and their delivery schedules. Every day, thinking, thinking.

Almost every day, I remind myself to read more letters from troubled friends. I try to respond to them all – sometimes all I can manage is a few lines, but I try to respect the fact that they chose me to share their troubles with, and I want to respond with compassionate words.

But here's where thinking has to stop. The thinking mind that has juggled appointment calendars, that has made shopping lists, and itemized invoices; that's not the mind that can respond compassionately to friends in need.

When I'm ready to write to someone who is hurting from grief, pain, or sadness, I have to go into my own state of flow. I have to leave my thinking mind behind and enter an altered state where my heart opens and the words pour out. When I write, it is a completely unconscious act. I have to trust my heart and my soul - trust that they can supply the words my mind cannot.

Here's an exercise you all can try. During one day next week, jot down your thoughts as they occur. It doesn't matter how trivial or how embarrassing; you don't have to show the list to anyone. Do this over and over again for a whole day. Then examine the list you have made. I bet you'll find something remarkable. Each of us actually has only a small set of thoughts that just keep recycling in our heads; kind of like our own personal top ten list. Sure, the specifics of successive thoughts change, but the templates are pretty standard.

Let me give you an example – thoughts of vanity. When a person frequently looks in the mirror to check their hair, their makeup, to check their clothes, or examine their figure. These thoughts – evaluating one's own appearance – are basically the same template. Some people recycle this family of thoughts through their heads thousands of times a day. Psychologists have a word for such a template – it's called a "meme."

After you have your collection of thoughts – go through them, sort them, categorize them into memes. It's a very humbling experience. You realize that most of your life consists of an automatic habitual meme dream. You realize that you're not what you thought you were. You thought you were deep and sensitive and profound and sympathetic; what you find is virtually all your mental energy has focused on twenty or thirty thoughts – over and over – most of them rather trivial or rather petty.

It's hard to look at because it creates a cognitive dissonance; you can see that you're not who you thought you were. So, what do you do? You look for the meaningful experiences beyond thought. Whether it's the orgasm or the touchdown, we start to put our faith in experiences that transcend thought, because we know deep down that the thoughts are not who we really are. It's when we're in the flow beyond thought that we finally experience our true selves.

In a way, this single principle probably accounts for 95% of human behavior. All the work, the saving of money, the investment in property; it's ultimately all about trying to create a few moments of transcendence in our lives. The man who drives 50 miles towing his sailboat, waits in line to launch it, maneuvers it into a secluded bay, and leans back to feel the gentle rocking of the waves and see the play of great white cumulus clouds against an azure sky – For a moment, he feels transported beyond thought. Even if it only lasts a few minutes, all the efforts that he made to create the conditions for this experience were worth it.'

The following day, Saturday, I conducted Eric's exercise for myself. It was a bit awkward stopping myself every few minutes to make notes about what I had just been thinking. But Eric was right – at the end of the day, I wasn't very proud of my list. For me, the thoughts on my list were about duty and about control: thinking about the duties that arose in my relationships with Eric and Cathy, and thoughts about how I could control how the future unfolded. As I perused my list, I had the distinct feeling of being stuck. I didn't like the narrow range of my daily thought patterns, but I also didn't know what to do about it – I didn't know how to enter the state of flow that Eric had described.

Chapter 16
Transformation

Life and death are of supreme importance.
Time swiftly passes by and opportunity is lost. Each of us
should strive to awaken.
Awaken! Take heed, do not squander your life.
by Eihei Dōgen

It was a hot August night, and even with the air conditioning, my bedroom was stuffy. I couldn't sleep. I kept glancing at my alarm clock and thinking about how tired I would be the next day at work.

At three o'clock I gave up trying to sleep. I pulled on my shorts and a t-shirt and went outside for a walk. As I walked past our house, I noticed a light through the basement window. Curious, I peeked in. It looked like I wasn't the only one who could not sleep. Eric was busy applying lacquer to one of his cabinets.

At breakfast, I was very tired. I didn't mention to Eric that I had seen him working in the middle of the night, but I was struck by how energetic he seemed. For someone who had not slept he was doing very well, indeed.

Over the next four nights, my insomnia continued and I went for more late-night walks. Every night Eric's light was on and he was either reading, meditating, playing the violin, or using the computer.

At breakfast I pressed him. "When do you sleep Eric? I've seen your working in the middle of the night all week long."

He glanced up from the newspaper he was reading.

"Actually, I haven't slept in months. Ever since I began meditating, my need for sleep has diminished. At first, I was sleeping four hours at night. But after a few weeks it fell to one hour a night. And since June, I have not slept at all. Sometimes, around four o'clock in the morning, I feel a little tired – but I just meditate for 10 minutes and am wide awake again.

The great thing about not sleeping, he said, was it freed up so much time that he could spend pursuing hobbies and reading. He had taught himself the violin and was learning to read Pali. He had reserved every night from 10 pm until 5 am to pursue special hobbies and interests. That's nearly 50 hours a week devoted to learning new things.

I enjoyed my own sleep, but I did feel a little envious of Eric. I later read that it is commonplace in Buddhist monasteries for the monks to sleep only a few hours per day. And in Buddhist legend, they say the Arhats – the awakened saints – never slept. In Buddhist doctrine, they say sleep is necessary to process mental defilements, and when the mind is purified, sleep is no longer necessary.

'Groundhog Day' was Eric's favorite movie. In the film, a curmudgeonly weatherman played by Bill Murray, Phil Connors, is sent to Punxsutawney, Pennsylvania. His assignment was to cover the annual festival that gave Groundhog Day its name. With great ceremony, town officials query a groundhog about his shadow, and announce somberly that six more weeks of winter are in store.

Phil Connors has soured on life; he is resentful toward what he considers a trivial assignment – so resentful it spills over into sarcastic remarks on live TV.

Then a miracle occurs. Phil Connors wakes up the next morning and it's Groundhog Day all over again. The day is an exact repeat of yesterday; people he meets say the same things to him; the same events occur. Of all the people in the world, only Phil is aware that the day is repeating over and over.

The movie chronicles Phil's life as he lives the same day, over and over, trapped in an endless cycle. He attempts suicide – to no avail. Then he takes piano lessons. While the rest of the world stands still, he gradually acquires the skill of a great musician. He amazes his colleagues with his new knowledge and skills. He gradually learns to use his predicament to his advantage, robbing banks with impunity, and manipulating people for his own gratification. Eventually he tires of it all. Finally, he uses his predicament for self-transformation.

Near the end of the movie, he announces "I've killed myself so many times, I don't even exist anymore." This is the turning point, leading him back into the stream of ordinary time.

Eric saw the movie as a spiritual metaphor. "We're all caught," he would say, "in an endless cycle of rebirths. We have to keep reliving our lives until we can extinguish the ego that pulls us along. We have to transform ourselves to escape. If you use this life to acquire things, to control, to seek power – guess what? You'll be back. Just like Phil in the movie, you'll be back to try it again. And you'll keep coming back until you realize what you were really here for in the first place – to transform and move on."

Chapter 17
Knowledge, Wisdom, and Samsara

*Beings are the owners of their karma, heir to their karma, born
of their karma, related through their karma, and have their
karma as their arbitrator.*
Karma is what creates distinctions among beings.
by Gautama Buddha

Nearly two years after The Circle had begun, Eric and I
had welcomed hundreds of visitors who came to our home
on Friday evenings. Mostly, they came with afflictions –
pain, grief, or sorrow, and they hoped to find healing in the
company of Eric and Sam Hill. Some Friday evenings, we
had as many as twelve visitors from San Francisco, Sausali-
to, Monterey and beyond – all of them had heard about us
from friends or acquaintances. We got phone calls and letters from many more, but we had to put them on a waiting list. Because of the limited size of our house, we limited attendance to twenty-two. By June 2000, The Circle had
grown to ten, including the Donovans, Eric, and myself.

This limited the number of visitors each week to twelve.
Eric and I took donations from everyone, both visitors and
members, to offset the cost of dinner. Nothing was charged
for the discourse that Eric gave following dinner – I guess
he was following the tradition set by U Bo Thet fifty years
earlier in Rangoon. The Dharma was free to anyone who
asked to attend.

Eric never rehearsed for Circle sessions and he never
used notes; he just entered the room with a deep sense of
presence. Sal, a member of The Circle, told me that the first

time he participated he couldn't get over the way that Eric looked at him. "I felt like Eric was looking right through my eyes, as if he was curious about who was in there behind my eyes." Sal's comment didn't surprise me; I had heard the same thing from others. I had the same experience talking to Eric, and I talked to him every day.

But what was going on? How was it that Eric affected people so deeply with just a minute or two of contact? I had minored in psychology in college and I remembered that both Freud and Jung had emphasized the importance of ego defenses. Freud explained that each of us makes adaptations in our personalities as we grow, suppressing aspects of ourselves that displease our parents, cultivating aspects that are praised and accepted.

We all carry a persona, a social self which we display to others, and a shadow self which we conceal, not only from others, but also from ourselves. Freud explained that we spend a major part of our lives engaged in behaviors to prop up the persona and keep the shadow hidden. Ego defenses eventually become so habitual that we lose awareness of them. We have long forgotten how to live except behind the armor of our chosen person.

When we meet Eric Hill, suddenly we are face to face with a guy who has no persona, no shadow, and no ego defenses. Eric is standing there with all his shields down, making his very soul completely accessible to anyone who wants to look. When he speaks, it comes straight from his heart; he seems very vulnerable at first, and then you realize there's nobody that he's trying to protect. People got high just being with him. It's kind of magical.

After listening to Eric, people realized that here's this young kid with a high school education who understands life and death. He operates from a vantage point deep within his soul where he responds in all the 'wrong' ways, compassion instead of envy, encouragement rather than competition, forbearance rather than anger. In Buddhism, these traits are called the *divine abidings* and it is believed that they take many lifetimes to cultivate.

Visitors were enthralled when they realized that Eric didn't fear death. I think for most of us, death is the big taboo – we live our lives in denial. But Eric had died so many times, it was like someone who has gone to the same vacation destination year after year. The idea of permanently moving there after retirement is not upsetting; after all, one knows the place intimately. That's how Eric felt about death; he had visited numerous times for years, he liked it, and had no concerns at all about permanent relocation. That's why talking about death with Eric was uplifting. He could talk about it with no hint of reactivity – just like others would talk about gardening or stamp collecting.

That's also the reason Eric was so effective volunteering at the Kindred Spirits Hospice. The patients were all terminally ill, and most of them had only weeks to live. Many were frightened; some were angry. Most looked terrible; their diseases had taken their toll. In the midst of all this suffering, the nurses and social workers tended to the patients' needs and tried to keep their spirits up – but the staff was also a little freaked. When you're surrounded by death every day, it can stir up fears of death within you. The staff would smile at the patients and act nonchalant, but the patients could sense the fear behind their smiles. When Eric visited, he would move easily among the patients – grasping hands, connecting with his eyes, praying with them, completely at ease in a room full of death. Patients were drawn to him not for what he possessed, but for what he lacked; and the thing he lacked was fear.

So, this is why during a particular Circle session, I chose to press Eric. I asked, "I know from watching you at the hospice that you're not afraid of death, but why? What do you know that we don't? Do you know if there's a God? Have you seen him? Can you describe him to us? Do you know that your soul is going to survive the death of your body?"

I felt a little embarrassed at my own bluntness, but I wanted to know, and I wanted Eric to explain it in words I could understand. Eric looked around the room for a few seconds and spoke softly.

'I don't know the answers to your questions. When I stop my heart, I briefly inhabit the consciousness of other beings who died long ago. I don't know whether these beings are myself in past lives – I do know there's karmic connection between us. And I know this connection between my life and the lives of these other beings stretches back in time over three millennia. I also know that this sequence doesn't end with me. One will be born after my death who will inherit this chain of connected lives. Whether he will remember them as I do, I don't know. But I know that all the beings in this long chain will exert an influence in him and will shape his character.

When I try to make sense of my mystical experiences, it's hard to find the right words. The words that seem to fit best are words from Theravada Buddhism. The Pali texts describe samsara, the never-ending wheel of birth, death, and rebirth. The texts discuss the mechanism of mind that causes this cycle of reincarnation. They suggest that a person can stop samsara, sort of like jumping off the wheel. But knowledge alone won't release you; only wisdom that comes from introspection will – you have to see the truth within yourself.

Looking deep within oneself takes a lot of courage because when you take a really penetrating look, you see that the true nature of the world is radically different from what you've always believed. This radical new truth is a frightening thing to acknowledge. Jung said, "...people imagine that the world is what we think...if you stepped beyond that picture you would cause an earthquake in the ordinary mind, the whole cosmos would be shaken, the most sacred conventions and hopes would be upset..."

There's a huge collusion in clinging to our customary, habitual picture of the world. And as long as we cling, we get reborn again and again. Clinging is the engine that propels us forward into rebirth. When we "step beyond" as Jung says, we stop clinging to our habitual picture of the world and the engine stalls; we are reborn no more.

I don't call myself a Buddhist, but when I read the Pali texts, I feel like I'm reading an account of my own experiences. It is as accurate as words can be.'

Chapter 18
Camping with an Attitude

*The greatest discovery of my generation is that human beings
can alter their lives by altering their attitudes of mind.*
by William James

When Eric was 24 his friend, Bruce, gave him some
camping equipment. Bruce had been an avid camper, and
had taught all four of his kids to enjoy the wilderness. But
Bruce's kids had grown into adults and had moved away.
Bruce's interest in camping had waned. So, on a Sunday afternoon in May, Eric brought home a truck full of Bruce's
sleeping bags, tents, camp stoves, lanterns, and other equipment. Eric was delighted by his windfall and spent the day
trying everything out: he lit the lanterns, pitched the tents
throughout the house, rolled and unrolled sleeping bags.

Then he told me that he wanted to go camping that
weekend.

"We can't go until Saturday – we've got The Circle on
Friday evening," I said.

Frankly, I wasn't too keen on going camping; my memories of camping as a kid consisted mainly of insect bites and
sunburn.

"Besides," I said, "the weather forecast is calling for rain
this weekend."

Eric looked delighted. "Perfect!" he said. "That means
the campgrounds won't be crowded."

I saw that he had made up his mind so I helped him
make calls to the members of The Circle. Eric wanted them
all to come camping. Of course, they had read the weather

report and were reluctant. But Eric persisted and was able to persuade all but two to come with us. Tom and Cathy Donovan didn't come, saying they had houseguests from out of town.

When I got home from work on Friday, Eric had already loaded up the van. The sky was darkening and flashes of distant lightening dotted the eastern sky.

"You're sure you want to do this?" I asked, clinging to a vain hope that he would come to his senses. He just smiled and patted my shoulder.

We picked up the others and drove two hours into the mountains. By the time we arrived, it was dusk and the rain was beating a steady rhythm against the roof of the van. Eric had reserved a campsite near the lake that was not accessible by car. So, we had to lug all the gear for a half-mile down a trail that had turned into a six-inch-deep river of mud. By the time we got the tents up and fire started, darkness had settled in.

As we gathered in a circle inside the large tent, Eric asked us how we were feeling. Naturally, we all said we were wet, cold, and uncomfortable. Eric asked us to join him in a prayer. He began a slow chant in Pali:

'Sabbe satta sada hontu
Avera sukhajivina
Katam punna-phalam mayham
Sabba bhagi bhavantu te'

This chant, he explained, was a central tenet of the Buddhist scriptures. Translated, it means:

'May all beings always live happily
Free from enmity.
May all share in the blessings
Springing from the good I have done.'

It took us a while to get the hang of reciting it in Pali, but after a few minutes we were in synch, slowly rolling the Pali words off of our tongues in unison. Then Eric asked us to visualize the people we loved – bring them clearly into our mind and hold their images as we recited it once more. Next we were asked to visualize acquaintances we did not know well. Again, visualize them and share blessings with them. Finally, he asked us to visualize people with whom we were having difficulties and repeat the chant again.

After the chant, Eric talked to us about how our egos prevent us from separating ourselves from the circumstances of our lives. Just as we adapt ourselves to the heat of summer and the cold of winter, we can live without anxiety if we release ourselves from the pull of our egos. With a smile, Eric suggested that pitching camp on a cold, rainy night was an opportunity for all of us to look at how our egos influence our lives.

'Too often, we see ourselves at odds with our life circumstances. A loved one dies, and we are lonely. We lose a job and become fearful about our future. We receive a gift and we feel valued; we lose something precious and we feel lost. Lived this way, life feels like a gamble. We might find ourselves in favorable circumstances and we might not.

Some people say that each of us creates the reality in which we live. They mean that everything, this tent, this campground, the other people in our lives, are all being manifested from our own mind. I don't know if that's true. I suspect that if it is true, it's occurring at a deep level that's inaccessible to all but the saints. What I do know is that each of us creates the attitude that we bring to reality. When we feel gloomy and disconsolate because it is raining and muddy, we're not aware that we are creating this negative attitude – it's a choice we have made. When we feel elated on a sparkling, clear, starlit night, we don't usually view our feeling as a choice, either. The usual way that people understand their feelings is as reactions to the circumstances of life, not choices.

Eric paused and then gazed at each camper in turn.

If you practice, you can start to notice how you create your own attitude minute-by-minute, day-by-day. Many monks start their day with the chant we were singing.

> *May all beings always live happily*
> *Free from enmity.*
> *May all share in the blessings*
> *Springing from the good I have done.*

What I love about this chant is that it helps us to cultivate an expansive sense of compassion for others and for ourselves. As we let go of our ego, we let go of our reactivity. Suddenly it's ok if it's winter and cold. It's ok if it's summer and hot. We can even cultivate a sense of joy as we slog through mud on a rainy night. Look up and feel the rain on your face. Take off your shoes and feel the mud oozing through your toes. Feel a part of nature's play.

Tomorrow I don't know what the weather will be – I can't control it. Whatever it is, it is. Whatever the weather, I can begin the day by creating a joyful attitude. If you're willing, I would ask that we all meditate at sunrise. It's a wonderful sense of freedom to take firm control of the one thing that we can control – our attitude about the new day. Then we can chant our Pali song and spread the blessings of the day to all beings great and small, near and far, seen and unseen. Then it won't matter what the weather brings.

I'm not sure how the other six processed the evening's talk, but for me it was really uplifting. The next day we all meditated and chanted together. When we chanted, I visualized everyone I knew, including someone at work with whom I was having difficulty. Just as Eric suggested, as the muscles in my body relaxed, I could also feel the grip of my own ego easing.

The next day was much better than the weather forecasters had predicted. There were a few scattered showers, but also some sunny interludes. We hiked, took pictures, and played scrabble near the campfire. I felt happy. And if it started to rain again – not a problem.

Chapter 19
Journey to Tibet

There was a time when meadow, grove, and stream,
The earth, and every common sight,
To me did seem
Appareled to celestial light,
The glory and the freshness of a dream.
From *Ode: Intimations of Immortality from Recollections of*
Early Childhood by William Wordsworth

In the spring of 2003, Eric began to contact another being named Khaydrup Je. Khaydrup Je was a 15th century Tibetan monk. Unlike U Bo Thet and Ananda, Khaydrup Je was a historically significant person whose life was recorded in history books about the rise of Tibetan Buddhism.

Khaydrup Je was the chief disciple of Tsongkhapa (1357-1419), the greatest spiritual leader of Tibet. Tsongkhapa was a child prodigy, taking ordination as a monk at age three. He spent a lifetime alternating between long meditation retreats, teaching, and writing. In 1398, at age 41, Tsongkhapa devoted the remainder of his life to helping others realize the goal he had attained. Under his guidance, thousands of other Tibetans also gained enlightenment, and a spiritual renaissance was launched in Tibet.

After Khaydrup Je ordained as a monk and became a disciple of the itinerant master Tsongkhapa, he dedicated himself to meditation and tantric rituals, putting forth relentless effort. But in 1409, as he approached his 30th year, he still had not attained the goal that his master had reached. That year Tsongkhapa took Khaydrup Je and 18 other disciples on a journey to the hot springs at Tolung, Tibet, a remote spiritual retreat. Under the moonlight near the steaming springs, Tsongkhapa gave a discourse on overcoming mental hindrances. Khaydrup Je sat very close to his master and listened intently. Midway through the discourse Tsongkhapa stood up and leaned against a large granite rock. His body, luminescent in the night, sank several inches into the hard granite. When Tsongkhapa took his seat again, an impression of his body remained in the rock, an impression that is still visible today.

For Khaydrup Je, seeing the master accomplish this miracle was a pivotal moment in his spiritual evolution. Instantly, he became a sotapatthi, established at the first level of awakening. Tsongkhapa prophesied that Khaydrup Je would be reborn seven more times and in his seventh incarnation would attain full enlightenment.

Eric contacted Khaydrup Je four times. On the first contact, Khaydrup Je was undergoing ordination at age 3. On the second contact, Eric was able to witness, through the eyes of Khaydrup Je, Tsongkhapa's miracle at Tohung. The third contact coincided with Tsongkhapa's death. The fourth and last contact found Khaydrup Je himself dying in the year 1470.

I was intrigued by these contacts because they spoke of specific landmarks that still exist today. The rock at Tolung and the monastery at Ganden can still be visited by the determined tourist.

After the last contact with Khaydrup Je, Eric seemed pensive. I think experiencing his spiritual origin so intensely and quickly, had significantly affected him. It wasn't often that I had spiritual advice for Eric, but this seemed the opportune moment for it. "Go to Tibet. You can visit the monastery; you can go to the hot springs of Tohung. You can get the completion that you need."

Eric looked at me, puzzled. He was unaccustomed to this role reversal. He grabbed my arm and squeezed it. "Sam, sometimes I need to be the student, and let you teach me. Let's make the arrangements. Let's go together next month."

Chapter 20
Messing with the Future

If it were done, when 'tis done, then 'twere well
It were done quickly. If th' assassination
Could trammel up the consequence, and catch
With his surcease, success: that but this blow
Might be the be-all and the end-all—here,
But here, upon this bank and shoal of time,
We'd jump the life to come.
From *Macbeth* by William Shakespeare

I had been watching Eric make contact with beings of the recent and distant past, and I had filled up volumes of transcripts with Eric's accounts of his adventures. Several times, I asked Eric whether he was just reliving past-life memories, or whether he was actually journeying into the past. For some reason, he shrugged off my question and said, "What difference does it make?"

It made a difference to me. If all Eric was experiencing were memories, then his contacts were not that different than some of my vivid memories of my childhood. Some of the best and worst experiences I had as a young boy were so indelibly etched in my mind that I could close my eyes and conjure up a vivid frame-by-frame memory. The same feelings and sensations that I had at age eight would come rushing back to me.

But I was under no delusion that I had accomplished time travel. These were just memories – I could relive them but I couldn't change them.

Eric's contacts in past lives had a slightly different quality. Eric said he felt his own will at work during the contacts. He spoke many times of influencing U Bo Thet's thoughts or actions. But from my philosophy studies in college I knew that, if true, what Eric said had enormous implications.

For example, on November 18, 1978, Peoples Temple leader Jim Jones instructed all members living in the Jonestown, Guyana compound to commit an act of 'revolutionary suicide,' by drinking poisoned punch. A total of 918 people died that day, nearly a third of whom were children. U Bo Thet died in March, 1977. If Eric was truly present in U Bo Thet's body in 1977, could he have issued a warning of the massacre to come and possibly prevented it? Or perhaps Eric could have warned President Carter about his ill-fated attempt to rescue American hostages held in Beirut in 1979? The possibilities are endless. He might have been able to have a positive influence on the future of the world.

I got a little annoyed at Eric for treating my question so dismissively, and so, one Saturday morning as we ate breakfast, I pressed him for a definite answer.

"Eric, it makes a difference what the nature of your contacts with these past lives is. If it's just a lucid memory, then together we're constructing a history of Eric Hill as he journeyed through multiple lifetimes. But if today's Eric Hill is journeying back to that past life and is actually present in the past time, it's a monumental event because it means you could potentially change history. And if you could, then why not do it? Why not prevent the Jonestown massacre? Surely the world would be better off if these events had been prevented."

Eric rolled his eyes and leaned back in his chair.

'I can see you're not going to give up on this, Sam. So, you win. I'll tell you what I know. I did influence U Bo Thet's behavior in

small ways. For example, I saw a newsstand in Rangoon in 1975. U Bo Thet was in a hurry, and had no intention of stopping to buy a paper. But my attention was on the headlines of that day's paper, and I wanted to read the article. It was about a fire that had taken place the night before, destroying a Buddhist temple.

I tried to direct U Bo Thet's attention toward the newsstand, but he was focused on getting to a medical meeting in Rangoon. He resisted and pressed ahead down the sidewalk. I continued my effort to will him back to the newsstand. For me, at this point it was no longer about the newspaper. I wanted to test precisely the question that you posed. I wanted to know if I could really change the past. I knew that without my presence, there is no way U Bo Thet would have turned around and returned to the newsstand. So, it came down to a test of wills.

I began concentrating intently, creating a visual image of the newspaper headline and projecting it outward into U Bo Thet's mind. U Bo Thet hesitated a couple times and, as I continued to press, he stopped completely, seemed momentarily puzzled, then smiled and turned around. He bought the paper and read it on the trolley car on his way home that afternoon.'

I was both fascinated and disappointed in Eric's account. Fascinated because Eric was finally confirming what I had suspected for years: that his trips were far more than recovered memories – that Eric really was transcending time. But disappointed that there was no way to verify it. The situation that Eric described was so trivial that no one would have noted it or remembered it. It would not have affected the future in any material way.

I asked, "Eric, can't you give me something more? If you're going to conduct an experiment, let it be something that you can verify after you return from the trip. You know, like burying a tin can full of money in the ground at a particular location so that upon returning to the present time, we could go to that same location and dig it up."

Eric was silent for almost a minute as he studied my face. His long pause made me uncomfortable. But with Eric, sometimes you just have to wait him out.

Finally, Eric sighed and said, "Do you remember how after Mom and Dad died, we sorted through their papers, separating the papers we needed, like his will and his life insurance, from all the rest of his stuff?"

I nodded and waited for him to continue. But instead, he excused himself and went upstairs. A minute later he was descending the stairs with a letter in his hand. He handed it to me. "This is a birthday card that I found in Dad's papers. I never told you about it, but I probably should have, since it's addressed to you."

I looked at the envelope. It bore a postmark from Rangoon, Burma with a date of April 9, 1975. I pulled the card out. I didn't recognize the handwriting.

> *Sam, I hope your second birthday is full of joy.*
> *I look forward to meeting you in a few years.*
> *Your Dharma friend,*
> *U Bo Thet*

Eric said,

'I had the same misgivings as you after the newsstand incident. I wanted to test my influence over U Bo Thet in a scientifically verifiable way. In the spring of 1975, two years before his death, I was able to write this card through U Bo Thet. I had to persuade U Bo Thet to relinquish control long enough to let me write. U Bo Thet experienced it as a kind of 'automatic writing'.

When the card was finished and the envelope addressed, my trip ended abruptly. The next time I tripped, several weeks had passed in U BoThet's life. I searched his thoughts, but couldn't ascertain whether the card had been mailed.

I thought later about asking Dad if he had ever received any strange letters from Burma, but the whole idea just seemed too crazy to pursue. I had convinced myself that my trips were, in fact, just memories. Incidents like the newsstand and the birthday card were just bits of my own imagination mingling with the memories. I had decided that there was no 'time trap' involved in my trips.

Then, as we were going through Dad's things after his funeral, I found the card from U Bo Thet. He had mailed it after all. And Dad had kept it all these years. Maybe he thought it was a prank. I don't know. But he kept it anyway and it's in your hand now. Proof that my trips are more than memories.'

My heart raced. "So, before you contacted U Bo Thet, this card didn't exist. And after your contact, the card existed. Now, after your contact, history has been altered. In this new history, the card had existed in Dad's dresser drawer since 1975."

Eric grinned. "Pretty awesome, huh?"

Chapter 21
What's a Soul Anyway?

As leaving aside worn-out garments
A man takes other, new ones,
So leaving aside worn-out bodies
To other, new ones goes the soul.
From *Bhageavad Gita*

Eric loved to talk about his soul. He was extremely curious. "What was his soul? Where did it start? When will it end?" He loved to toss out such questions to anyone that would listen.

I listened, but I didn't have any good answers. In Sunday School I was taught that I had an immortal soul; but never really knew what that meant. I went on to obtain a Bachelor's and Master's degree in Religious Studies, and still didn't know.

I think my images of soul are conditioned by Hollywood movies like 'Heaven Can Wait,' 'Ghost,' and 'What Dreams May Come.' In such movies, the soul is depicted in human form – the same form that it had before death, and with the same personality and memory. The soul, however, is distinguished from its human predecessor by a halo of light and by supernormal powers. Of course, I know this is a childish conception of soul. To carry so much of oneself into the afterlife would be not unlike moving to Indiana; same self, different location.

Eric had this uncanny ability to ask simple questions that were hard to answer. So, I directed the question back to Eric: "You are the one that died a hundred times. You tell us about your soul."

I had a tape recorder on for this session, so I have a transcript of the discourse that followed.

'What's wrong with believing that the soul is our personality? After all, that's what most people recognize as 'myself.' The personality that likes pizza and babies; the personality that detests hip hop music and sweltering August days; the personality that enjoys screaming at football games, arguing about politics, and driving fast cars; the personality that remembers romantic moments and tries to forget past shames. What's wrong with the view that, after death, our personality looks down from heaven with all the same thoughts and feelings, likes and dislikes, that constituted 'me' when I was alive?

Stated thus, most people will reject that description of soul. But I would ask, if not that personality, then what? What exactly constitutes the soul? Does the soul retain the good qualities like love and compassion, and cast off the bad qualities, such as jealousy and anger? Is the soul just the positive fragment of the personality, split from the rest? Maybe that's closer, but it's still not quite right.

Most people don't know what they mean when they refer to their own soul. And therein lies a paradox. On the one hand, people say that the most important goal of their life is to save their soul, and in the next breath they will acknowledge they're not sure what this soul is.

What I'm suggesting is that people acquaint themselves with their own soul. Spend time with your soul, explore it, commune with it, feel its pres-

ence. Feel within yourself the difference between soul and personality; know the part of yourself that is deathless, and know the part of yourself that is destined to die.

Part of the reason that we are strangers to our own souls is the culture in which we were raised. Our western scientific culture tells us that all understanding comes from externalizing. Whether we want to count the dimples in a golf ball, measure the mass of an electron, or calculate the orbit of a planet – the method is the same. We have subject and object; observer and observed. We understand all things by assuming a position of observer apart from the phenomenon that we're observing; we're not the golf ball, we're not the electron, and we're not the planet.

But we can't observe our soul that way. Because the soul is not "out there." It can't be externalized. The soul can only be visited through union – by merging the observer with the observed. This introspective path is the only way to discover the deathless part within each of us. What we learn by union of the seer and the seen cannot easily be verified, measured, or replicated; it fails to qualify as scientific knowledge and – in our culture, it therefore fails to be knowledge at all.

I guess that's the reason so many people in the west are embracing the religions of the East; they know, at a deep level, how spiritually impoverished the scientific world view leaves us; they want to recapture the mystical life that our culture has robbed from us.'

Chapter 22
Mugged!

Better to conquer yourself than others.
When you've trained yourself, living in constant self-control,
neither a deva nor gandhabba, nor a Mara banded with Brah-
mas, could turn that triumph back into defeat.
From *The Dhammapada*

Cathy and I went out to dinner on a Tuesday in the summer of 2004. The Italian café was just eight blocks from home and the evening was cool, so we walked. We dined on spaghetti and Chianti and talked about the little details of our lives. It felt good to have a conversation that was just focused on the banalities of everyday life. Conversations with Eric seemed to have such a philosophical tone, and it was nice to just chatter away without having to concentrate on big or abstract ideas.

We continued to chat as we strolled home. There's an alley between 6th Street and Sutton Place that we walked through in order to reach the restaurant. It's home to a dumpster and the associated odors, but it does shave a block off the walk. It was dark, and Cathy and I instinctively hesitated before turning into the alley. Inside the alley there was a light burning over the rear entrance to a store and no signs of danger, so we turned in and resumed our previous conversation. Just a few seconds later, our lives changed.

A man stepped out from behind the dumpster, pointed a gun at us, and demanded our money. I froze in place and time seemed to stand still. I glanced at Cathy and saw she was gripped in fear. After the initial shock, I pulled my wallet out and tossed it on the ground at the man's feet. Cathy did the same with her purse. The man bent over to pick up both, keeping his eyes on us except for an instant. When he stood up again, he was the one that looked as though he were gripped by fear. His eyes widened and he uttered a frightened moan. He seemed to be looking past us and, instinctively, I glanced behind me but saw nothing. He dropped my wallet and Cathy's purse back on the ground and began retreating from the alley, walking backwards, bumping into trashcans, and muttering over and over, "I'm sorry. I'm sorry."

I was very confused, but also relieved that he was leaving. At the same time, I kept seeing glimpses of someone else in the alley with us through my peripheral vision. I would sense some movement out of the corner of my eye, but when I turned my head no one was there. Cathy and I picked up our possessions, exited the alley from the opposite end, and hailed a cab to take us home.

When I got home, we were both still shaken. I called the police to report the crime, and they said they would send an officer over to take a statement. Then we told the whole story to Eric. He didn't seem the least bit alarmed; in fact, as we finished the story, he had an amused smile on his face. He said, "So you met Michael."

"What? Who's Michael? What are you talking about?" I felt angry that Cathy and I had nearly gotten killed, and here's Eric smiling and talking in riddles. Before I could retort, Eric explained who Michael was.

"In every religion on earth," Eric said, "there are unseen beings."

He sat on the floor and motioned for us to join him. Somehow the process of gathering on the floor had a calming effect on both Cathy and me. Eric continued.

'I've always had this ability to stop my heart at will, and that has allowed me to explore death and past lives. It's been an incredible journey for me. But from it all, I was never certain what it meant. About six months ago, I died and visited U Bo Thet again. It was my 100th contact with him and also my last. He was very ill and I think he was within a few days of death. As I looked through his eyes, I could see his wife and friends had gathered by his bedside. They all seemed so full of compassion.

In every contact I had with U Bo Thet for the last 10 years, he had gotten progressively older. My aging was tied to his aging. Now that he was dying, I knew there would be no more contact. As I looked out over the room, one of the visitors stood out from the rest. To my surprise, he seemed to lack solidity – I could actually see through his body to the wall behind him. U Bo Thet smiled and greeted him, calling him Michael. When he did, I saw the other visitors look at one another, but not at Michael. I realized that U Bo Thet and I were the only ones who could see this visitor. I sensed that Madam Thu and his friends thought U Bo Thet was having hallucinations from his illness.

But I could see that it was no hallucination. In spite of his illness and his weakened body, U Bo Thet was still quite lucid and alert. As my thoughts merged with his, I learned that U Bo Thet had befriended an angel – or as U Bo Thet called him, a "Deva."

Buddhists believe that there are many beings that share the world with us, but who cannot ordinarily be seen. Two kinds of beings, 'Devas' and 'Brahmas,' live on higher planes of existence. They live in planes of light and energy, but absent of matter. It is believed that especially virtuous people may be reincarnated as Devas. In fact, a famous passage from the Pali Canon says:

"But those who in the noble Dharma
Are endowed with acceptance and inner peace.

When they discard the human body
Will fill up the heavenly hosts of devas."

For the Buddha, meetings with Devas and Brahmas were a common occurrence. The first conversation that Buddha had after his enlightenment was with the Brahma Apatta, who persuaded the Buddha to become a teacher. Buddha had a close relationship with the Sakka, the Deva King. When the Buddha fell ill with dysentery, Sakka came and nursed him back to health.

When a monk finishes meditating, he says, "Whatever merit I have gained (through meditation) I freely share with all the Devas and Brahmas." These beings find it difficult to meditate and are grateful when humans share the benefits of meditation with them. The Devas watch over and protect the humans who share merits with them.

U Bo Thet, like all the people in Burma, was taught to believe in Devas and Brahmas, but he never saw one until he was dying. I felt so happy to be in the presence of this Deva that I didn't want to leave. I felt like Michael was aware of my presence, and when he spoke, he confirmed my feeling. He said, "Eric, your time with U Bo Thet is ending, your time with me begins." When he finished his sentence, I awoke with a shudder here in my own room. I looked around the room and there, sitting on my bed, was Michael.

Since that day, Michael visits me at least once every day, and he told me he watches over both you and me continuously. I've learned a great deal from him. I have lost any wish to stop my heart again – I feel that all I need I can find here and now with you, with The Circle, and with Michael.

Now, returning to the frightening experience that you and Cathy had tonight: I was here in the house talking to Michael when he suddenly looked startled. He told me that you were in distress and he vanished. Ten minutes later, I saw the cab pull up to the house and let you and Cathy out. I didn't know what had happened to you, but I knew you had a Deva looking out for you.'

I leaned forward and touched Eric's shoulder. "Please thank Michael for us."

Later that night, when we were in bed, Cathy asked me if I really believed Eric's story. I told her I wasn't sure. I thought I had seen someone or something with us during the mugging, and it sure seemed like the robber saw something that frightened him.

I didn't tell Cathy that I was worried about Eric. The Deva, Michael, had only appeared to U Bo Thet in the final weeks of his life. Did Michael's appearance in Eric's life signify that Eric would soon die? I tried to reason my concern away; *It makes no sense*, I thought.

"Eric's only 28 years old and he's in good health."

Chapter 23
Madam Thu

*Since there actually is another world (any world other than the
present human one,
i.e. different rebirth realms),
one who holds the view 'there is no other world' has wrong
view...*
From *Apannaka Sutta, Majjhima Nikaya*
by Gautama Buddha

As much as I admired my brother, I held some doubts
about his mystical exploits. I mean, how could anyone be
sure that his recollection of past lives was not just the product of his imagination? It was the same skepticism that
I held towards some of the so-called 'channels' that plied
their trade up and down the west coast. These channels
would enter a trance and, supposedly, a spirit entity would
occupy their bodies and speak through them. I saw several channels either in person or on video, and nothing they
ever said or did seemed other than ordinary. I mean if they
talked in ancient Sanskrit while levitating six feet off the
floor, one would at least entertain the idea that they were
really channeling, but when they just spouted pop psychology that anyone could read in the self-help section of the
bookstore, the whole premise was unconvincing.

I didn't think Eric was a charlatan. He was the most spiritual person I knew. He was incredibly insightful and eloquent. And I think he believed everything he said. But I felt
there were other plausible explanations for what he did, explanations other than reincarnation and past life memory.

This was my state of mind three years ago when Tom Donovan called me on the phone, clearly excited. "Can you come to our house right away?" He didn't want to explain over the phone. Fifteen minutes later I was sitting in the Donovans' living room with Tom, Cathy, and two Burmese women. Tom told me the whole story.

'When Cathy and I took our summer vacation to Thailand, we spent three days in Rangoon, Burma. We went to different government record offices asking about U Bo Thet. We had no luck, but our tour guide took us to a public library where the Rangoon paper was archived and indexed. We found three articles on U Bo Thet – all dealing with his work in the community as a meditation teacher. Apparently, when he wasn't working as a doctor, he taught small classes in his home. The articles indicated that he would often have 22 people at his home on Sundays, practicing Anapanna and Vipassana. U Bo Thet never charged for his services, saying that the Dharma should always be given freely.

Each of the articles gave his address in Rangoon and mentioned his wife Daw Ma Thu, or Madam Thu. One of the articles was an obituary. The date of his death was February 28, 1977.

We found U Bo Thet's home on a small and quiet tree-lined street in a northern suburb of Rangoon. A knock on the front door brought Lin to the door. (Tom indicated the younger of the two women sitting opposite me was Lin.) We first asked if she was the widow of U Bo Thet. She laughed and said no; she was U Bo Thet's niece. She told us that Madam Thu was upstairs.

We struggled to explain our purpose, and we were apparently not very successful, as Lin looked quite perplexed. She did offer, however, to summon her aunt. We went into the parlor, the same room that U Bo Thet had used for his meditation classes.

A few minutes later, Lin returned with Madam Thu (Tom gestured toward the elderly Burmese woman.) Madam Thu

seemed to understand us better than Lin, but she also looked ex-
tremely skeptical. She asked us if there was any specific informa-
tion Eric had given about U Bo Thet, and we rattled off a series
of facts: that he was a doctor, that he was married, that he was a
meditation teacher.

Madam Thu laughed and told us that many people in Ran-
goon knew that much about U Bo Thet. I told Madam Thu that if
she were willing, I would like her and her niece to come to Amer-
ica as my guests. I offered to pay all expenses. I only asked that
she meet with Eric once and see for herself whether Eric's stories
were true.

At first she politely declined, but I kept pleading. She final-
ly relented. Two days later, all four of us were in the first-class
cabin on United Airlines, flying back to San Francisco. We finally
arrived home just an hour ago.'

I'm not sure what motivated Tom Donovan to begin inves-
tigating Eric's past lives. I suspect he wanted to scientifically
validate Eric's experiences by finding out about the real U
Bo Thet. Now that I knew what Tom had done, I was just
as excited as he was. Maybe we had the proof we needed to
erase any doubts about the authenticity of Eric's tales.

I called Eric and told him that we were bringing 'his
wife' to The Circle this evening. He seemed to know what
I meant, saying "Don't tell me that you have Madam Thu
with you!" Eric said he was going to prepare a special dish
for her.

Tom and I had another hour to chat with Madam Thu
before she and her niece went upstairs to rest. I asked Madam Thu if she recalled any item of personal information
that was known by her and U Bo Thet, but by no other person. At first she said no; she gestured to Lin, saying that her
niece took care of her now, and she had no secrets from Lin.

But after a minute, she did remember one thing.

"U Bo Thet and I never had children of our own, Madam Thu said. "All our relatives hoped we would have a family, and we made up a reason why we didn't. We said that I was unable to bear children. But that was not true. There was actually another reason I wished not to have children. I told the reason to U Bo Thet alone, and made him promise to tell no one else."

"Don't tell us, either," said Tom. This will serve as a test for Eric.

As I drove home to help Eric prepare for that night's Circle, I recalled the date that Tom had given for U Bo Thet's death – February 28, 1977. Eric's birthday was January 4, 1978– almost exactly nine months later.

The rest of The Circle had already arrived when the Donovans came with Madam Thu and Lin. Eric was delighted to meet them. He began conversing with Madam Thu in halting and fragmentary Burmese, but Madam Thu seemed to have no trouble understanding him and smiled broadly. We had dinner and Madam Thu pointed to the dessert Eric had made and said that it was her favorite dish.

After dinner we gathered in a circle and Eric told Madam Thu the entire story about his contacts with her late husband. He spoke in English now and Lin translated. Madam Thu listened attentively, nodding her head occasionally, but otherwise seemed reserved in her judgment. There was a pause when Eric finished; I interjected, telling everyone, "Madam Thu told us that only she and U Bo Thet know the reason they didn't have children."

Eric smiled. "And U Bo Thet also promised never to reveal the real reason. Are you prepared to release him now from that promise?"

Madam Thu's interest seemed piqued. "Yes, yes, he is released."

Eric leaned forward in his chair and gazed intently at the hardwood floor below. Although it was uncharacteristic of him to look away when he spoke, he maintained his focus on the floor as he began.

'When Madam Thu was fifteen years old, she had a terrible and vivid nightmare. She dreamed that she was married and had a daughter who had been brutally raped and murdered. In the dream, she experienced unbearable pain and grief over the loss of her only child. She awoke and was haunted by this dream for the rest of the day. Years later, when she and U Bo Thet discussed having a child, the same nightmare recurred. Madam Thu took it as a bad omen, and U Bo Thet concurred. They resolved to have no children so the dream could never become real.'

It took a minute for Lin to translate Eric's response, but when she had, Madam Thu was clearly shocked. Her hand flew up to cover her mouth and her eyes began to water.

"It's true," she gasped.

Tom Donovan and I glanced at each other. He looked glum, and I think I know why. He was feeling as guilty as I was. We had both succumbed to the seduction of the scientific approach. But the whole journey with Eric wasn't about science; it was about spirit. It was about the big questions that science couldn't answer. Our experiment didn't prove or disprove anything.

Oddly, Eric and Madam Thu remained politely distant for the rest of the visit. I had thought they might treat the day as a poignant reunion. But apparently, Eric's revelation had not altered the fact that she and Eric were still strangers, from different lands and different generations.

That night, as I lay in bed, I wondered what it all meant.

Was Eric U Bo Thet – or just a person who happens to share U Bo Thet's memories? I can't remember any past lives. Is that the same as not having any? If I ever met Mom or Dad or Eric in another form, would I recognize them? And what would I say?

Chapter 24
Saying Goodbye

In the long, sleepless watches of the night,
A gentle face--the face of one long dead--
Looks at me from the wall, where round its head
The night-lamp casts a halo of pale light.
From *The Cross of Snow,* by Henry Wadsworth Longfellow

By September, Eric had lost over 60 pounds and was quite frail. He didn't leave the house anymore. He would sit and read for an hour or two, and then fall asleep. On September 14, he asked me to set up the video camera for him. I complied, positioned the camera on the tripod, and focused it on Eric, who was sitting cross-legged on the floor. I had no idea what he had in mind. At first, he just stared at the camera for about five minutes, his eyes were open wide and exceptionally clear. Then he began a slow lyrical chant. It wasn't in English; it sounded like an Asian language to me – I thought perhaps Hindi. I figured he was reciting a poem that he had memorized during one of his trips. The chant went on for 30 minutes, punctuated by occasional pauses where Eric would stare at the camera while he caught his breath. When he was done, he quietly asked me to shut the camera off.

"Put the file somewhere safe," he instructed. "Eventually a friend will come and ask for it. When he comes, you must give it to him."

"When...who?" I asked. "How will I know this person?"

"Don't worry," Eric said. "You'll know. But it may be some years before he comes."

I copied the file and tucked the USB flash drive in the back of my dresser drawer. When I returned to the living room, Eric was still on the floor. "I'm taking another trip now. This is going to be my last trip." I took a sharp breath. Even though I knew this day had to come, tears welled up in my eyes and I felt a convulsing in my throat and chest. I also knew it was pointless to argue. I got my cushion and seated myself facing him. He reached over and caressed my face. "Thank you, Sam. We'll see each other again." With that, he closed his eyes and died for the last time.

I sat and sobbed quietly for ten minutes or so, with my eyes closed. Every time I opened my eyes and saw Eric's body, a new wave of grief swept over me. Then something extraordinary happened. I felt like all the tears had been drained from me. My sobbing subsided, and I felt a warm rush of energy through my body. I opened my eyes wide, and there, sitting right next to Eric was a ghost! He was an old man with long grey shoulder length hair, a thin face with a long nose, and what looked like a deep scar across one cheek. But he was not solid – I could see through him to the wall behind. He was a shadowy, translucent being. I blinked, thinking my tears were causing a hallucination, but he was still there – very real, very vivid, and smiling at me. Then it struck me – I was looking at Michael. When I began to move Michael's form began to dissipate and, in a moment, he was gone.

I went upstairs to lie down on my bed. I thought I would wait a few hours before calling Eric's friends and telling them.

We had to drive deep into the woods to build a funeral pyre for Eric. One of Eric's friends owned some rural property near the Russian River. He showed us a clearing on his property nearly a quarter mile away from the closest neighbor. Here, we could cremate Eric and scatter his ashes.

About 200 people came, all twenty of Eric's inner circle and nearly all the residents of Blackbird Court. Five of the hospice patients were too ill to travel, and they stayed behind with a nurse. Aunt Rose came from Idaho, as did Eric's high school shop teacher. We didn't publicize his death in advance of the funeral. Frankly, I didn't want a big mob of people at my brother's funeral. But word leaked out, and about 150 people came from around the country. People who had been healed by Eric at one time, and people who had never forgotten – a large crowd, but not too large. Eric would not have wanted too many. These were all people who felt deeply privileged to have been part of Eric's unusual life.

In her eulogy, Cathy said, "I am blessed beyond words by the Brothers Hill. I look back on my two years living and working with Eric Hill – a gift precious beyond measure. And I look forward to my future with Sam – another precious gift still unfolding."

I had written my own eulogy for Eric, but kept choking up when I tried to read it. I finally quit trying. I think everyone knew what I was trying to say.

For two years after his death, members of The Circle continued to meet at my house every Friday evening. Cathy and I prepared dinner for all who came. After dinner, I would play one of Eric's Dharma talks on tape. But tape recordings weren't the same as Eric in person. The uncanny stillness that would descend on the room when Eric talked didn't occur with tapes. Gradually, attendance at The Circle dwindled. Cathy and I were disappointed but not surprised. Sandy and David moved to Detroit. Max passed away the following winter. Sue and Frank retired and bought a small winery in the Napa Valley. For the remaining members, we began holding The Circle just once a month, on the first Friday, but by 2011, Circle dinners often consisted of just Cathy and me. The next year, even Cathy withdrew, saying she wanted to spend Friday evenings in her upstairs studio, painting. I still treat Friday evenings as sacred time. I like to play the last 5 minutes of Eric's final words. I have no idea what Eric is saying, but that doesn't matter. It is still the most poignant communication from Eric for me.

Cathy continued to teach at Sedalia Elementary School. We never married, but everyone in the neighborhood believed we were husband and wife. We didn't correct them. We both assumed that we would get married one day. It just didn't seem like a priority.

Cathy and I stopped our volunteer work for Triple Refuge in 2012. I had worked nonstop for 12 years and Cathy for 8 years. By 2002, the Foundation had enough active volunteers, enough sponsors and benefactors, and enough of a reputation to assure its long-term success. I still serve as an honorary member of the Board of Trustees, but that only requires me to attend a two-hour meeting every three months.

Cathy and I settled into a comfortable, if predictable life. When we weren't at our jobs, our time was structured around dogs, meditation and art. We adopted two Labrador Retriever puppies who sprawl across the bed with us at night. Cathy meditates with me, even though it's not her favorite thing; I paint with her, even though it's not my favorite thing. We take a month-long vacation every summer at Shanti Springs, where we rent a small cottage. And we enjoy reading, going to movies, and eating dinner at the Golden Thai Café. It's owned and operated by our friend and former Circle member, Maria Gomez. Each time we go, she insists on preparing something special for us, saying "It's small payment for the magical Fridays I spent at your house."

For the last year, Cathy has been telling me she's ready for a career change. "It's not that I don't like teaching." She said resolutely. "It's just that sixteen years is enough time for any job." I told her there was no need for her to work at all. With my pension from the Postal Service and my savings, we have more than enough.

"I don't work for money – I work because I want to," she snapped. "Work shapes my life. It gives me an identity."

I never felt that way about my work. I spent twenty-five years as a computer specialist with the U.S. Postal Service. I admit, I enjoyed writing computer programs, testing them, and seeing them work. But I hated the endless meetings that I had to sit through. I enjoyed the camaraderie of some friends at work. But I hated the Christmas parties and company picnics that I felt obligated to attend. I never identified with my job. For me working was a contract – trading my time for my salary. When the Postal Service began to downsize, my opportunity came. With the summers that I had worked during high school and college, plus twenty-three years of full-time employment, I was eligible for early retirement. I walked out of the Santa Clara Postal Annex for the last time on August 2, 2018. I was happy – and free.

Last month, one of Cathy's resumes finally bore fruit. She was offered a job with the State Park Service in Sacramento, a job where she can care for the environment instead of thirty-two young children. It's the job she's dreamed about for quite a while.

She asked if I would move to Sacramento with her. Her

excitement was contagious and I found myself agreeing immediately. But later that night, when I was alone in my study, the excitement evaporated. Why did I agree so readily? I was born in this house, the same house my parents bought so many years before. I had never moved anywhere in my entire life.

Chapter 25
Noble Paths and Golden Doors

It's a drum and arms waving.
It's a bonfire at midnight on the top edge of a hill,
This meeting again with you.
by Rumi

No one had ever come for the video like Eric predicted. It had sat untouched in my drawer for over nine years.

Then, exactly one week after donating our house to Triple Refuge, at 2:30 in the afternoon, the doorbell rang. I opened the front door and encountered a slight man with piercing blue eyes, a fringe of short white hair surrounding his otherwise bald head, and an envelope clutched tightly in his hand. He looked at me tentatively and asked, "Hello, are you Sam Hill?" I nodded. "Well, I have a letter for you from your brother, Eric." He raised his arm and released the

tight clutch on his envelope. Even as I reached out to take it, I could see the handwriting on the envelope was Eric's.

"Who are you?" I ran my fingers gently across the envelope while keeping my eyes focused on this stranger. He looked vaguely familiar.

"I don't know if you remember me, but I was

a friend of Eric's. My name is Stanley Summers." I stared blankly; I did not recognize his face or his name.

"About thirteen years, ago, I was a patient in the hospice across the street, Kindred Spirits. I remember you and Eric would come on Sundays to visit with all the patients."

I did remember – Eric and I would spend two hours there every Sunday afternoon – but I still didn't remember Stanley.

He continued. "Well I was very close to death, and I was in pain. Eric was very kind. He sat on the edge of my bed and his voice was the most comforting thing I had experienced in months. As we talked, I told him I was a Buddhist and that I had practiced meditation for many years. He sat with me while we meditated together. As I meditated with Eric, I could feel my pain begin to melt. When he left after ten minutes, I was searching my body, trying to figure out where the pain had gone."

I ushered Stanley into the house. He settled into the green armchair next to the fireplace and continued. "One week after meditating with Eric, I was in remission. Two weeks after that, I had regained my normal weight and was released from Kindred Spirits."

Now I remembered him. His hair had receded; there were fine wrinkles around his eyes and mouth, and the glasses were new – but I remembered him. He was the only person to ever be discharged alive from Kindred Spirits. At the hospice we healed hearts, and souls, and minds; but Stanley was the only who was healed in body.

I invited him in. I hesitated, because I really wanted to read Eric's letter, and I wanted to read it in private. But the letter had waited thirteen years to be read; another fifteen minutes would not matter.

"Why did you wait so long to give this to me?" I motioned for him to sit on the living room sofa.

"That was Eric's instruction. You can see it on the envelope. He wrote, 'Deliver on January 11, 2019.' He was very specific. He also told me that you would have something. Something that he made."

I looked at the envelope. Following the delivery instructions, Eric had signed and dated the envelope. "Stanley, did you know that Eric passed away a few days after he gave this to you?"

"Yes, he told me when he gave me the letter that he was dying. That was why it was so important that I promise him to make the future delivery."

I rummaged around in the cupboard drawer and located the USB flash drive. I was actually hoping Stanley would take it and go. I wanted to be alone to read Eric's letter but Stanley stood in place, scrutinizing it.

I decided to be gracious. "Would you like to watch the video now? You can play it on my computer over there." I motioned across the room.

"Yes please." I took the flash drive from him and inserted it into my computer, feeling slightly annoyed that Eric's letter would have to wait.

It had been several years since I had watched the video. The poem, chanted by Eric in flawless Pali, was still captivating. I became absorbed once again and forgot about Stanley, who sat just a few feet away. When the video ended, I turned to him. He was sitting very still and his eyes were open in a blank stare. Rising from my chair to touch his shoulder, I realized he was quite dead.

His hands and face were cold and he had no pulse at all. My heart raced. The obvious explanation was that Stanley had simply died. He had somehow cheated death before, but it had caught up with him. But I had a deep sense that something else was happening. Could it be that Stanley had the same gift as Eric?

A few seconds later, I had my answer. Stanley's body shook and he spoke with slow but certain words, "That was incredible." He began rubbing his hands together to remove the chill.

"You mean this is the first time this has happened to you?"

"Yes. The video is a sort of instruction manual. It's in Pali and is sung in metaphorical verse. It took me a few minutes to comprehend that the chant, about noble paths and golden doors, was a guide to conscious dying. To really hear it, I began meditating as I listened. I let the words resonate in my mind without trying to analyze them. The chant's true meaning can only be grasped in a meditative state."

Stanley rose from his seat. "I should go. You have a letter to read, and I have a life to live." He pressed his palms together and bowed to me. I returned the gesture and walked him to the door. I watched as he started his car and drove away. Then I sat on the living room floor and breathed deeply four times. I opened the letter.

> *Dear Sam,*
>
> *I know you're a bit confused as you read this. I hope Stanley is doing well – I was glad to help him with his healing. When I met him at the hospice, I could see that he was dying but also sensed that it wasn't his time. He still had important work to accomplish. I intervened, weaving my own karma with his. I knew that after Stanley recovered and contin-*

ued to meditate, he would reach a point where he could undertake the deepest teachings. I left the video for him. The Pali chant that I recorded is about a golden door. It explains what the door is, how to approach it, how to go through it, and how to return. It's hard to describe the process explicitly. I hope my ode made sense to Stanley.

I realized as I worked with Stanley that my own time was drawing to a close. Stanley could stay; but I had to depart. I didn't trade my life for Stanley's. It's just a matter of timing. Like Stanley, I have important work to accomplish. But the critical work is in my next life. I have to undertake a task in 25 years for which I am still unprepared. My next birth will prepare me.

As I meditated during the last month of my life, my visions changed. I was joining life with an adolescent boy. The experience was not as lucid as my experiences with U Bo Thet, Ananda, and Khaydrup Je. Everything seemed obscured by a bluish haze. I struggled to see and to make out the voices of others.

At first, I thought the quality of visions was just deteriorating due to my illness and my weakened body. But then I caught a glimpse of a Time magazine cover – the date was December, 2019, thirteen years in the future! It occurred to me that the haziness of the vision had nothing to do with my weakened state; it had to do with the still tentative nature of future reality.

The adolescent boy walking through the blue haze is me in my next life. I connected with him in three different meditations. The first time, I overheard my parents speaking French – and I could sense that it was their usual conversational language. I regretted never taking any French courses in high school; I couldn't make out what they were saying. But I could see their accent was odd – they were not speaking traditional French, but some kind of dialect.

When my father answered the telephone, he switched to English. I gathered from his conversation on the phone that he was a baker since he was discussing the delivery schedule for a large order of croissants. That explained the aromas of freshly baked bread that wafted through the apartment. Either he baked in his home, or his home was near the bakery.

On the second contact, I was able to locate the place better. A copy of the New Orleans Times-Picayune was on the coffee table. Suddenly, the oddness of my parents' accent became clear, they were speaking Cajun! I looked outside the window, hoping I would see a definite landmark, like a store name, or a street sign. It was not to be. My contact evaporated.

The final time I connected with this adolescent boy, he was entering church with his parents. A Catholic church, made of stone, with four high steeples. The contact lasted only a moment.

I don't know if this is enough for you to locate me. I can't even say whether I'm in New Orleans, since the Times-Picayune is read throughout Louisiana.

In three days, I'm going to die for the last time, and to commemorate the occasion, Michael is going to make himself visible to you! I hope you enjoy meeting him. If you turn the page, I have a final gift for you. I drew a pen-and-ink portrait of Michael. If you look for me, bring this picture along. Maybe it will help me remember who I am.

    Love always,

    Eric

I paused for a few seconds before I turned the page, and then quickly looked. There, stapled to the letter, was a richly detailed ink drawing of a man's face. It was identical to the being I saw in the minutes after Eric's death. Not just a resemblance – the hair, the eyes, even the large scar on his cheek – an exact image of what I had seen.

As I looked at the drawing, tingling heat swept through my body. For a minute, it felt like my body had become energy. I saw a rapid sequence of visions, like a kaleidoscope. I didn't fight the experience. In fact, I relaxed and let the energy course through me from head to foot. When it finally subsided, I tentatively began to move my arms, gradually reorienting my shaken body. When it was over, I felt transformed. As I looked around the room, I was looking through new eyes. I felt a deep sense of calm.

In the following days, I noticed that I was reacting and responding differently to the circumstances of life. All the things in my life that I used to prize: my house, my car, and my books – now felt like encumbrances.

Buddhists believe the path to enlightenment has four stages. The first stage is called 'stream enterer', or in Pali – 'Sothapatti.' Becoming a sothapatti, one gains faith beyond doubt. The extinction of doubt is the foundation for proceeding to higher stages of enlightenment. It took a few days before I could find the word to describe my transformation. But now I believe that, as I sat on the floor of my living room on a September evening and looked at Eric's drawing, I became a Sothapatti. After many lifetimes, and with the help of my gifted younger brother, I had entered the stream. I owe so much to Eric, and if I can find the right 12-year-old boy living over a bakery in Louisiana, I will thank him.

www.ingramcontent.com/pod-product-compliance
Lightning Source LLC
Chambersburg PA
CBHW060438180626
46817CB00007B/2871